DARE
TO
Dream

ESSENCE BESTSELLING AUTHOR

DONNA
HILL

ARABESQUE®

Recycling programs
for this product may
not exist in your area.

DARE TO DREAM

ISBN-13: 978-0-373-53478-4

Copyright © 2012 by Donna Hill

First published by BET Publications, LLC in 2004

www.kimanipress.com

Printed in U.S.A.

Acknowledgments

Many thanks to Andree Michelle
for her help with the background on Sag Harbor,
but especially for introducing me to the
incredible information on the Grenning Gallery.

Dear Reader,

Thank you for purchasing *Dare to Dream,* a love story that will hopefully sweep you away. I loved crafting my heroine Desiree, a strong-willed, creative young woman who is challenged on every level to regain her sense of self after losing everything. Of course, no love story would be complete without the perfect man—Lincoln Davenport— who fits the bill from head to toe. And he is determined to have Desiree—no matter what.

When I was writing this novel, I had the pleasure of spending time in the Hamptons in Sag Harbor, New York, doing "research." Many of the scenes are peppered with real places, people and streets mixed in with a bit of my imagination. I had such a wonderful experience there that it led me to write *Heart's Reward* in 2010, where I first introduced readers to Melanie Harte and her family and my edible hero Rafe Lawson, who of course is the to-die-for bachelor in my Lawsons of Louisiana series. Needless to say, I couldn't seem to shake my love of Sag Harbor, so much so that I will be introducing a new series, Sag Harbor Village, which debuts with a new novel this fall! You'll see some of your favorite characters from my previous books and meet some new ones. Perhaps by that time, Rafe Lawson will have settled down—or maybe not! In the meantime, please enjoy Desiree and Lincoln's wonderful story and let me know what you think.

You can always find me on Facebook, www.facebook.com/donnahillfans, or on Twitter, www.twitter.com/donnahill, and you can always send me an email at dhassistant@gmail.com. I promise to answer.

Until next time,

Donna

Chapter 1

"Desi, Carl Hampton is here to see you. He said he wanted to check on the progress of your paintings for the exhibit. I told him you were busy."

Desiree Armstrong sighed loudly and mumbled a curse under her breath. With great reluctance she put her paintbrush down and turned to her assistant.

"Thanks, Cynthia." She wiped her hands on her once-upon-a-time white smock that was now mottled in an array of rainbow colors. "One of these days I'm going to make enough money to host my own exhibition. Sponsors seem to have this crazy notion that the artist has nothing better to do than be at their beck and call." She stood and rolled her stiff shoulders. "How does he ever expect me to finish my work for the show if he 'drops by to see my progress' every fifteen minutes?"

They both laughed.

"Tell him I'll be right down. Let me get cleaned up and make myself semi-presentable."

"Hey, take your time. If he really wants to see you, he'll just have to wait, now, won't he?"

"You got that right."

Cynthia turned to leave the studio, her waist-length, honey-blond hair swinging behind her.

Desiree smiled as she headed toward the industrial sink set off to the right side of the studio loft. She and Cynthia had hooked up and become fast friends when Desiree was teaching an art course at Pratt Institute in Brooklyn. Cynthia had a keen eye for what was good and what wasn't, but her artistic talents stopped cold right there. But rather than leave a profession she loved, she signed on as Desiree's assistant and they'd been together ever since. That was five years ago, a time when Desiree desperately needed a friend. A time when she was struggling with the reality that Lincoln Davenport, the man she'd given her heart to, would never be hers. With her best friend and soror Rachel Givens heavily involved in her own life and love, Cynthia proved that she could be the ear and the shoulder Desiree needed.

Lincoln. Funny, she hadn't thought of him in at least a week, in some form or the other. She turned on the water full blast and grabbed a bar of brown soap. That was a good sign, she thought as she briskly washed her hands with the precision of a surgeon. Maybe soon she could say two weeks, then three, and finally never.

She dried her hands on the towel hanging from a nail by the sink, pulled the smock over her head and smoothed out her badly wrinkled denim shirt. "Too bad." She tsked and marched downstairs into the intimate gallery that bore her name. She put on her best smile when Carl turned to greet her.

"Desiree, so sorry to tear you away from your work."

"Hmm. How are you, Carl?"

"Anxious." He grinned. "The show is only a couple of months away. I simply wanted to check on my investment."

Desiree placed a hand on her hip and cocked her head to the side. "Carl, you know I really appreciate your support. There is no way that I would be able to host a show myself. But…"

"But what?" He stepped closer and the scent of his cologne wafted around her like a morning mist—clinging.

Briefly she lowered her head, then looked him straight in the eye. "The thing is, Carl, the more you stop by, the longer it takes me to get finished. I have seven more paintings to complete. I need the time to concentrate. I can't do that if I am…interrupted."

He reached out and stroked her chin with the tip of his index finger. Desiree struggled not to recoil.

"I would think that a few moments of your time

with me would be worth it. After all, we are partners, Desiree."

The last thing she wanted to hear today was that, without him, the exhibit wouldn't be possible. Something nasty was right on the tip of her tongue when the bell over the door rang. "Excuse me, Carl, I have a customer."

Carl clasped her arm, halting her departure. "Why don't you let Cynthia get it? That's what she's paid for, isn't it?"

"So am I," she said and walked away.

His eyes narrowed as he watched her charm the woman who'd come in, talking and laughing as if they were old friends. Carl slid his hands into the pants pockets of his imported Italian suit, then leaned against a counter and monitored the exchange. Everything about Desiree Armstrong was a work of art, from the soft spirals of her hair to the slender figure that even a model would envy, the eyes that danced with images that only she could see and skin reminiscent of the finest brandy and just as tempting to look at. There was no need for him to "check on" her progress. If he knew nothing else about Desiree it was that she was the consummate professional, dedicated to her craft with a single-mindedness that was almost frightening to watch. Yet, it was the only excuse he could fathom to bring him to her door and into her presence. He was certain that with time and money, she would be his. He was a patient and very wealthy man.

* * *

While Desiree talked to her client as they walked around the shop, she silently prayed that Carl would get tired of waiting and leave. Every day she regretted having signed the agreement allowing him to sponsor her exhibit. She'd always prided herself on being her own woman, not beholden to anyone or anything but her craft. But the sagging economy had made it extremely difficult for anyone trying to survive in the arts. If it had not been for Carl she would have lost her studio, her gallery such as it was and any chance of having her own show. Now she was stuck and it was growing more apparent by the day that Carl wanted much more from her than a few of her etchings.

"Thank you for your business, Ms. McKay. I can have the piece sent to your home if you wish."

"No, that won't be necessary."

"Cash or charge?"

"Cash," said Ms. McKay. She pulled out her wallet. "But I'd really appreciate it if you could wrap it really pretty. It's a gift for my daughter. She's moving into her first apartment."

Desiree reached beneath the counter and pulled out a roll of gold foil wrapping paper. "That must be exciting," she said.

"Exciting for her, but sad for me. I have a bad case of empty-nest syndrome already." She laughed lightly.

"You'll be fine. Living in New York, you'll find

plenty to keep you busy. Before you know it, you'll be redecorating her room!"

"I'll keep that in mind," she said, taking the wrapped parcel and another look around. "Thanks so much. Maybe I'll stop in again."

"Please do. And feel free to bring friends."

She smiled. "I certainly will." She glanced at the countertop and noticed the oversized postcard. "Oh, a gallery exhibit."

"Yes. Mine," Desiree said. "Late September."

Ms. McKay picked up the card and tucked it in her purse. "I'll put it on my calendar."

"Bring friends," Desiree called out as the woman left. She took a breath and silently prayed that Carl would be preparing to leave. But upon looking in his direction she realized her prayer had gone unanswered. She put her smile in place and walked over to where he stood.

"I really need to get back in the studio and try to finish up, Carl."

"Wouldn't you like some company?"

"That wouldn't be a good idea."

He cleared his throat. "Well, you have to eat sometime. Why don't I come by about eight and we can—"

"Carl." She held her palms up. "Look, I really appreciate everything that you're doing for me with this exhibit. I really do. But all we have is a business arrangement. Nothing more. And when these paintings sell, I'll pay you back every dime that you invested."

"I don't want your money, Desiree. I thought I made that clear."

She raised her chin. "Unfortunately, Carl, that's all I can offer you."

"Desi! Telephone," Cynthia called out from the front desk.

"Thanks. I'll be right there." She turned back to Carl. "I really have to go."

"Fine. But this isn't finished, Desiree. As you may have gathered by now, I'm a very determined man." With that he turned and walked out.

Desiree let out a sigh and headed toward the front desk. "Who's on the phone?"

"No one. You looked like you needed rescuing. I dialed the front desk from my cell phone."

Desiree shook her head and laughed. "Thanks. Look, I'm going back up to see if I can get my head back into what I was doing. Close up when you're done."

"Sure. I'll see you tomorrow. Need anything before I go? Want me to order some food?"

"Hmm, no, thanks. Maybe I'll order something later. See ya."

Upstairs in her studio, Desiree put on her smock and returned to her unfinished work. It was an abstract of 125th Street in Harlem back in the bebop days, complete with strings of nightclubs and men and women dressed in the finery of the era. It was almost the way she wanted it, but not quite. She picked up the brush, dipped it in the electric-blue paint that was her signature color and went to work.

The next time she looked up it was nearly 2:00 a.m. Her eyes were burning, her fingers were stiff and she'd swear her back was locked in a permanently hunched-over position. Slowly she stood and felt every muscle in her body scream in agony. She'd been sitting in the same spot for nearly nine hours straight. But when she sat back and looked at what she had accomplished, every ounce of pain was worth it. This was her best piece yet. She'd put her foot in it, as the folks would say. If it wasn't so late she'd call Rachel, the one person other than Cynthia who could understand her elation, her pride. But it would have to keep until tomorrow.

Desiree picked up the canvas from the easel and carried it across the expansive room to the other row of paintings that were in various degrees of drying. Some she would return to and add some additional touches, maybe another layer, others were fine as they were, while a few just didn't make the grade—at least in her mind.

She turned out the light on that side of the loft, took a quick shower and crawled into bed. If she wanted to put in a full day tomorrow she'd have to be up by six. Barely four hours of sleep, but she would do what needed to be done. Her dream was within the palm of her hand and she had no intention of losing her grasp on it. Her work was all she had since she'd walked out of Lincoln's life. She'd claimed that he could not compete with her real love—her art. How many nights had she lain awake on the fence of indecision: let him go and simply pursue her dream or cling to him and lose a part of her soul? Or—tell him the truth? She'd made her choice. Yet, the idea of them as one was never more than a whisper away from her thoughts.

As she drifted off to sleep, unwanted images of Lincoln danced in and out of her head. She tried to force them away, send them back where they belonged, but she was too tired to fight them any longer and finally drifted off to sleep with her and Lincoln dancing under the moonlight.

Sometime during the night, the light from the moon turned a blazing brilliant red, the clouds turned thick and black, choking her, seeming to enter her pores and fill her lungs. The cool evening turned warm… warmer, until her skin felt as if it were baking beneath the desert sun. The stars became blazing flashes of lights, spinning, and the sounds of her and Lincoln's laughter turned to screams and wails. She tried to open her eyes and couldn't, the black clouds were too thick, blinding her. She couldn't breathe as the room grew hotter. Coughing and gagging, she struggled to get up in the darkness as the horror of what was happening engulfed her.

Fire! Fire was everywhere. Flames leaped from the doorway, blocking her escape as they ran across the ceiling, licking the beams like a hungry lover. She lifted her gown to her face to cover her nose and mouth and stumbled blindly toward the windows, banging in futility against the reinforced glass.

She crawled along the floor, searching for a pocket of air, praying that someone would find her, get her out of this hell. Tears, mixed with terror and black soot, slid down her cheeks. The last thing she remembered before everything went totally black was a thunderous crash, the sound of breaking glass, and then nothing.

Chapter 2

"Desi, Desi... Can you hear me, sweetheart?"

Desiree struggled toward the sound of the familiar voice, hoping that it would finally lead her toward safety. The air in her lungs was still short and choppy, her throat and her eyes burned. But if she could just make it to the voice she knew she would be okay.

She forced her eyes open, certain that all she would see was darkness, thick black clouds and flames. Instead, everything around her was a pristine white and the figures wavering in her line of vision appeared filmy as if they were covered in plastic. Was this heaven?

"She's awake!"

There were sounds of running feet and unfamiliar

voices, authoritative voices, calling out instructions. The film was pulled away and pinpoints of light were flashed in her eyes. Something was covering her mouth, keeping her from speaking.

"Just relax, Ms. Armstrong," a soothing male voice said. "You've been through a traumatic ordeal. I'm Dr. Bernard. You're in the hospital. You're going to be fine. Do you understand me? Just nod your head."

Desiree slowly nodded.

"Good. You've been asleep for two days. We have you on oxygen. There was some damage to your lungs from the smoke. Some minor burns and cuts, but nothing that time and rest won't heal." He smiled and glanced over his shoulder, then back at his patient. "Your friend is here to see you. She's been here since you were brought in. I'll give her a little time and then I want you to rest."

Desiree nodded again, as tears spilled from her eyes. She was alive.

Rachel stepped into her line of vision. A gentle smile trembled around her mouth. "Damn, girl, if you wanted some attention all you had to do was call a sistah." Her attempt at holding back her own tears of relief were useless as they flowed unchecked down her high cheeks. She sniffed hard and wiped her eyes with the back of her hand. "Thought I'd lost you."

Desiree tried to talk over the oxygen mask but coughed instead.

"Just relax, okay? I know you're stubborn, but do as the doctors say so you can get the hell outta here."

"My s…tudio," Desiree managed in a harsh whisper.

Rachel momentarily lowered her gaze. "Everything is gone, sweetie."

Desiree squeezed her eyes shut as the enormity of what had transpired taunted her behind her lids.

"The important thing, Desi, is that you're here. All that stuff could never replace you. You can do it again. Even better next time."

She shook her head and began thrashing violently. "No," she croaked. "No."

"Nurse! Nurse! Relax, Desi. Please. Nurse!"

A nurse came rushing in followed by Dr. Bernard.

"I'm sorry, you're going to have to leave. I'll need to sedate her," Dr. Bernard said, stepping around her to Desiree's bedside.

Rachel slowly backed out of the room, covering her mouth to contain her sobs as she watched the surreal scene unfolding in front of her.

Out in the hallway she leaned against the wall and shut her eyes. If anyone knew how important Desiree's work was, it was she. She'd watched her struggle to build her career from nothing to opening her own small shop, spending hours toiling over the perfect combination of colors and form, teaching an art class to poor inner-city kids on weekends to help make ends meet. She was at a major turning point in her career, and now this. Everything she'd worked for up in flames. Gone forever.

"She's resting now."

Rachel opened her eyes to look into Dr. Bernard's. She swallowed hard. "Thank you."

He put his hand on her shoulder. "Your friend will be okay. The emotional shock is much more devastating than any of her physical problems. That will take time. I understand that she lost everything, even a place to live. Is there somewhere she can stay when she's released?"

"Of course. She can stay with me."

"Good. She'll need a friend. It may be best for her to get away for a while."

Rachel nodded her head. "When do you think she can go home—I mean be released?"

"Depending on her progress, a day or two."

"I'll be here."

"Good night. Try to get some rest."

Rachel watched as the doctor walked away, made a stop at the nurses' station, then continued down the hallway. Taking a deep breath of resolve, she headed toward the elevator just as Cynthia got off.

"Oh, Rachel. Hi." She tossed her hair over her shoulder. "How is she?"

Rachel smiled. "She woke up."

Cynthia grabbed Rachel in a bear hug and they both giggled and jumped up and down. When Cynthia stepped back, there were tears in her ocean-blue eyes.

"Thank goodness," she murmured, pressing her hand to her chest. "But what are the doctors saying? Is she… really okay?"

Rachel recapped what Dr. Bernard said.

The delighted expression on Cynthia's face slowly diminished by degrees. "Yeah, I guess that's to be expected. That studio, her work…" She looked Rachel in the eye. "They meant everything to her. And now…"

"I know. But Desi is tough. She will get through this and she'll be even stronger when she comes out on the other side. She just needs some time to pull herself together."

Cynthia nodded, then her eyes widened in alarm. "What is going to happen with the exhibit? It's barely two months away. All the preparation…the money." She pressed the heel of her palm to her forehead and clenched her teeth. "And Carl Hampton…he's going to go ballistic if he hasn't already. As a matter of fact, I'm surprised he's not all over the place like a rash, throwing his weight and his money around." She gave an exaggerated shiver. "He just rubs me the wrong way."

"Well, Desi certainly doesn't need to be annoyed by Carl right now. Maybe it's best that he does stay away, at least for the time being." She checked her watch. "Listen, I've gotta run. They gave her a sedative, she got a little upset, so I'm not sure if she is awake. But why don't you go on in?"

"Thanks. I just want her to know I'm here."

"Okay. Take care." She stepped onto the elevator just before the doors slid shut.

Chapter 3

"You know you're welcome to stay here as long as you need to, girl," Rachel said as she put Desiree's belongings in the guest bedroom. "And as soon as you get your strength back we'll go on a shopping spree like we used to do back at Howard." She laughed lightly at the college memory, but got no response from Desiree.

Desiree wandered over to the canopy bed, sat down on the side and stared out the window. The world didn't look any different than it had only days ago, she thought. People still moved along as if nothing at all had changed, as if her life and all that she'd lived for hadn't been destroyed. Couples still walked hand in hand, children still laughed and played, police still wailed their sirens, the sun still rose and set. It was all unreal to her. A part of her mind could not handle the information, because she knew differently. She knew that nothing was the same and never would be again. All she had left were the borrowed clothes on her back and a new toothbrush for all her years of struggle and sacrifice. A tear of desolation slid down her cheek. She covered her face as the sudden onslaught of sobs shook her body.

"Desi…" Rachel was immediately at her side, gathering her in her arms. "It's going to be all right. I swear it will. All that stuff is replaceable. I know you're aching inside, but imagine the world without you in it." She hugged her tighter.

"I…I haven't felt this kind of emptiness since…Lincoln." She wiped at her eyes and sniffed hard. "After him, all I had was my work. I poured all the love I had for Lincoln into building my shop, painting, and…my first show." She stifled a sob. "Now I have nothing." She turned to look into the eyes of her friend. "Nothing, Rae."

Rachel squeezed her eyes shut as she pulled Desiree against her shoulder. Her own heart ached for her friend. All she could do was try to help her through this crisis. Desiree was a strong woman, resilient. All she needed was time to get her feet back under her, and Rachel promised herself that she would do whatever was necessary to make sure she did.

Desiree wandered around Rachel's apartment like a ghost for the next week, barely speaking or eating.

She refused to see Carl at all and when Cynthia came to visit she hardly acknowledged her presence.

"She doesn't seem to be getting any better," Cynthia said as she sat in the kitchen with Rachel sipping on a cup of herbal tea. "Maybe she needs to…you know…see someone."

Rachel frowned. "You mean a shrink?"

"Yes. Maybe it would help. She certainly can't stay like this. It's not healthy."

"Desiree doesn't need a shrink, she needs to get her spirit back. I've seen her go through this before. She's healing, in her own way, and when she's ready she will come out of it. I know Desi, nothing will move her until she's ready to move."

"Well, not to change subjects, but she needs to really start thinking about her business, the show, finding a way to repay Carl. I can only hold him off for so long."

Rachel took a deep breath and nodded her head. "She will when she's ready."

Cynthia stood. "It really needs to be soon." She picked up her purse from the oak table. "Take care. And thanks for the tea."

Rachel didn't bother to walk her to the door. To tell the truth she was glad she was leaving. Cynthia might very well have Desiree's best interests at heart, but Rachel had never really cared for Cynthia. She simply tolerated her because of Desiree, who swore she couldn't run things without her, that she was indispensable. What Rachel really believed was that Cynthia was a no-talent artist who happened to fall into Desiree's lap at a very vulnerable time in her life and decided to latch on to Desi's coattails. Maybe the real truth was that she was a bit jealous of Desi and Cynthia's relationship, she grudgingly admitted. Cynthia had been there for Desiree when she really needed someone— that someone should have been Rachel. But she'd been dealing with her own issues at the time. Building her accessory-design business had taken her out of New York for months on end. She was virtually living in Europe when the fiasco with Lincoln had taken place, not to mention her affair with her Italian lover Claudio, and her on-again off-again relationship with Lucas Scott, which almost consumed her.

Sighing, she pushed herself up from the table. Maybe that's why she was trying so hard with Desiree, not only because she wanted to see her better, but also to assuage her guilty conscience.

She walked to the dishwasher and put the teacups and saucers in.

"Rae."

Rachel jumped at the sudden sound of her name, grabbed her chest and turned. "Girl, you scared me out of my panties. Whew." She closed the door to the dishwasher. "Hungry? I was going to fix something."

"No, actually, I was wondering if you would mind coming with me to the loft."

Rachel's thinly tapered brows rose in surprise. "The loft?"

Desiree nodded. "I think it's time."

Rachel took a deep breath and a slow smile spread across her face. "Yeah, it is."

When Rachel pulled up in front of what was left of the loft, Desiree's heart nearly stopped. All of the windows were broken out, debris was everywhere, the remnants of her gallery and paintings were piled in a sooty heap against the front door—destroyed. There was yellow caution tape surrounding the building. It looked exactly like what it was—a disaster.

"Do you want to go in?" Rachel asked with hesitation.

Desiree nodded and slowly got out of the car. She walked toward the entrance and looked up at what had once been her apartment. A chilling flash of that night and the terror she felt raced through her. And for the first time she fully understood just how lucky she really was. She hadn't been spared to spend the rest of her life wallowing in self-pity, she concluded. She'd been given a chance—maybe to start over, live her life differently, change her focus—she wasn't sure, at least not yet. But she was certain that she'd been spared for a reason.

She turned to Rachel. "I don't need to go in. There's nothing for me in there."

Rachel placed her hand on Desiree's shoulder. "Are you sure?"

"It's the first thing I've been sure about in weeks. Let's go."

* * *

Desiree was deathly quiet on the trip back. When they returned to Rachel's apartment Desiree took a seat on the couch. "Let's talk," she said.

Rachel took off her red leather jacket and hung it on the coatrack in the foyer. "Sure. What's up?"

"I know I've been a real pain in the ass these past few weeks. And you've been a really good babysitter. But it's time for me to get out of here and for you to get back to your life."

"Desi, you have not been a problem. That's what friends are for."

She nodded. "And I truly appreciate it. But it's time."

"Where will you go? What will you do?"

Desiree heaved a deep sigh. "I was thinking of going out to the shore for the rest of the summer. Get my thoughts back in order, maybe rekindle an old spark of creativity." She flashed a weak smile. "What do you think?"

"I think if that's what you need to do, then you should do it. But where? Actually you could stay at my place in Highland Beach. They're still doing renovations, but you would pretty much have the place to yourself."

"No. I've imposed on you enough. And I certainly don't want to be in the way of workmen."

"I guess you're right. So where to then?"

"I was thinking Sag Harbor. It's always so beautiful there this time of year. Remember when all of the sorors 'summered' there during our senior year at Howard?" she asked, affecting an aristocratic accent.

Rachel laughed at the memory. "Yes, the Alpha Delta X did their thing that summer. It is lovely there. Great shops, wonderful restaurants, and it's peaceful. Maybe you could rent a cottage or something."

Desiree nodded as the idea began to take shape in her mind.

Rachel leaned forward, excitement brightening her eyes. "If you go, it has to be under one condition."

Desiree's brows drew together. "What?"

"You let this be my treat. I'll arrange for everything. You won't have a thing to worry about."

"Rae...I couldn't."

"You can and you will." She folded her arms and pressed her lips together.

Desiree looked at Rachel and knew from the set expression of her eyes and mouth that no was not an option. "Okay."

"I'll take care of it tomorrow. And then we go shopping!"

Desiree laughed for the first time in weeks, and tomorrow suddenly didn't seem like such a bad thing at all.

Chapter 4

Carl Hampton entered the office building on Madison Avenue in midtown Manhattan and stepped onto the elevator. Hampton Inc. was located on the twentieth floor of the turn-of-the-century building and boasted an incredible view of the Big Apple, one of the reasons he'd chosen the location nearly fifteen years earlier.

Since he launched his investment company, he'd seen the country's unstable economy topple one business after another. But one thing he'd learned early on was to diversify. His assets and his sights were set on an array of enterprises and opportunities, and he'd amassed enough money to live the way he wanted. It also allowed him to indulge in his pet passion—art. The white-walled reception area of Hampton Inc. was lined with original artwork from around the world. Each of the dozen offices housed at least one treasured piece.

The elevator door opened and his receptionist, Denise, jumped to attention.

"Good morning, Mr. Hampton."

He murmured something in his throat and breezed by her.

Jake Foxx, one of his investment brokers, stopped him in the corridor.

"Carl, we really need to talk. The lawyers and the accountants need to know what you want to do about that loft thing. We need to get the papers filed and decide what to do with the property."

Carl cut his eyes at Jake. "Do you think that perhaps I can get into my office before you bombard me with what *you* need?" he asked with deadly calm. "I pay the accountants, the lawyers and you to take care of things. So take care of them." He walked off and into his office, slamming the door behind him.

He knew part of the reason for his ill temper was that he had not been able to talk to or see Desiree. It was eating him alive. He was sure that by now she would have contacted him, asking for his help. But not a word, not a call. How could she not need him?

He slammed his briefcase on top of his desk, sending a flurry of papers to the floor. This was not how things were supposed to be. Desiree should have been his by now. Hadn't he shown her how much he cared? Hadn't he provided for her every need? She'd come to her senses and realize what a fool she'd been to turn her back on him. The building, the exhibit, none of it mattered. The only thing that made a difference in his life was Desiree, and he had to find a way to finally make her understand that.

"Sorry, ma'am, we're full and probably will be for the next two weeks. You can try us back then."

"Thanks." Rachel sighed and hung up the phone. She'd called every bed-and-breakfast on Sag Harbor and received the same response: "Full, please call back." Short of going out there herself and scouting the places, she didn't know what else to do.

She leaned back in her chair and massaged her temples. She couldn't let Desiree down, not after all the huffing and puffing she'd done, swearing that she would take care of everything.

Running out of options, Rachel decided to call the tourist bureau. After about twenty minutes, the very patient and thorough customer service rep was ready to fax over information on a relatively new B and B called The Port.

"Thank you so much. You've saved a life today," Rachel said. "Yes, the fax is coming through right now. Thank you again. Have a great day."

Rachel hung up and hurried across the room of her home office to the fax machine. Each of the pages highlighted the attributes of this little-known treasure on Sag Harbor. Even though the picture of the resort was a bit grainy, she could tell that it would be perfect for

Desi. It offered all the amenities and provided the privacy that she needed while still giving her easy access to the rest of the affluent African-American community.

Before the last page was spewed out, Rachel was on the phone.

"Hello, please tell me that you have rooms available," she said, a bit breathless.

The deep voice chuckled. "Actually you're in luck."

"Oh, thank goodness. I'd like to make reservations— for the rest of the summer if that's possible."

"The rest of the summer works for us," he said. "We'll be happy to accommodate you."

"Actually it's not for me. It's for a friend. She really needs to get away, rest, and…well, she needs to get away. But I'll be taking care of all the bills."

"Not a problem. Let me put the guest clerk on the phone and she will take care of all the particulars."

"Oh…but can't you take the information? I've been on the phone for hours. I swear if I talk to one more person today I might snap."

"It can't be that bad," he said, keeping his voice light. The last thing he needed was an unhappy customer before she even arrived. As one of the newest establishments on the shore, he was conscious of building a solid reputation for customer service. "Trust me, the clerk will help you. I only own the place. I leave the running of The Port to the staff. It's important. I'm sure you can understand that. So please hang on and we'll get you all set up in no time at all."

Rachel rolled her eyes and sighed as she listened to the recorded music of Nancy Wilson. *At least it's not Musak,* she thought.

"Hi. I'm sorry to keep you waiting. My name is Terri. Tell me what you need and we'll make it happen."

Rachel gave Terri all the information and insisted that Desiree be given as much privacy as possible.

"We always respect all of our guests' privacy, so you don't have anything to worry about."

"Great. Put all the charges on my credit card. She's not to be bothered with anything."

"Understood." Terri took down all the credit information. "All done. We'll be expecting Ms. Armstrong on Sunday. And don't worry about check-in times, her room will be ready whenever she arrives."

Rachel exhaled a long sigh of relief. "Thank you so much."

"Not a problem. Have a great day." Terri hung up the phone and started to file away the reservation card.

"So who is our mystery guest this weekend, Terri?"

Terri turned in the direction of her boss's voice. "A Desiree Armstrong." She handed the reservation card to him.

It took a moment for the name and the reality to register, and when it did his breath stopped in his chest.

Lincoln blindly handed the card back to her.

"Are you all right, Mr. Davenport?"

"Uh, yes. I'm fine." He cleared his throat. "See to it that Ms. Armstrong has whatever she needs." He turned and walked away.

Lincoln stepped outside and stood on the porch of the main house, gazing out toward the sun that was slowly descending over the still waters. Orange and gold sunbeams streamed out across the slight ripples like pathways leading to eternity. For an instant, Lincoln wished he could simply put one foot in front of the other, step onto the guiding beams of light and walk off into the horizon. It seemed possible, almost preferable to having to confront the unimaginable.

Desiree. Even now, five years later, the mere thought of her made his heart race and desire heat his blood. Was this some cruel joke, some twist of fate that was bringing her here of all places? In three days he would know. But what then? What could they possibly say to each other to make what had gone so wrong right again?

Chapter 5

"I don't know how to thank you, Rae."

"You can thank me by relaxing and getting your head and spirit clear," Rachel said as she sped along Route 79 en route to Sag Harbor.

Desiree sat back against the plush beige leather of the Volvo and took in the sights as they unfolded along the highway.

Everything was in bloom, alive. Had this been any other time in her life she'd be reaching for her sketchbook and pencils to begin detailing all that her eyes could see or imagine. But this wasn't any of those other times. As much as she'd tried to put on a good face for Rachel and Cynthia, the truth was—she'd lost it. She'd lost her desire to paint. The inspiration that drove her to sit long, agonizing hours to bring her vision to the canvas or to a piece of clay was gone. And that realization saddened her as only one other thing ever had.

She hoped that this time away would somehow revive her passion, or at the very least give her a reason to pick up the fragments of her life.

Each time she closed her eyes she had nightmares, terrifying visions of that night, and she'd wake up shaking and soaking wet. She was afraid to be alone and ashamed to be around anyone. Now instead of the scents of turpentine and paint revitalizing her as they once did, they only evoked twisted memories, making her stomach revolt.

Everyone thought of her as "so together," strong, resilient, able to handle anything. But she was none of those things. Maybe at one time, but now she felt as if she were only a shell of the woman she once was. Would she ever be all right again? Ever? Would the constant fear that hung in the center of her chest ever go away?

Inadvertently a shuddering sigh rushed up from her chest and escaped across her lips.

"Desi? Are you okay?" Rachel quickly glanced in her mirrors, then eased the car onto the shoulder. "What's wrong?"

"Rae, I…feel so lost, like I'm drifting. I have nightmares every night. I can't paint, I can't think…" She covered her mouth with her hand.

"Desi." She clasped her left shoulder. "It's going to

be okay. You just need some time. You've been through a trying ordeal. Anyone who'd been in your place would feel the same way."

Desiree sniffed hard and reached in the glove compartment for a tissue. She dabbed at her eyes. "I know. I keep telling myself that," she said and wiped her nose. "Some days it helps and other days it doesn't."

"Are you sure you want to go to the shore? You know you can stay with me. Maybe it's too early for you to be alone."

"I'll be okay. I have to be. I know I can't keep living like this every day." She turned and looked at Rachel. "I just can't, Rae." She tugged in a deep breath and forced herself to smile. "I didn't let you come all this way for nothing. Let's go."

Lincoln strolled across the grounds behind his property, gravel and sand crunching beneath his sneakered feet, and walked toward the water. From his vantage on the hill, he could see for miles across the cloudless sky. The water was a soothing blue and moved in gentle ripples along the shoreline, seeming to meet the deeper blue of the heavens in a seamless line along the horizon. In the distance the white sails of the private boats could be seen flapping in the late summer breeze.

When he'd stumbled across the abandoned site four years earlier, he immediately saw its potential.

The eight cabins were nestled among manicured bushes, imposing gray rocks and a brook that ran in a crisscross pattern throughout the two-mile stretch of grass and sand. The main house was a stone's throw away from the water, and from its vantage point on the high hill it was a fairy-tale view at night.

But all that potential took work to be realized. What were now luxury cabins with all of the latest amenities had been shaped from a series of eight shacks in desperate need of repair. Everything from new plumbing to walls and new roofs were part of the renovations.

Yet with all the extras, the cabins still maintained an intimate, homey feel to them that his guests loved.

The Port had become his balm, a place to soothe his soul, a place to immerse himself in his efforts to get over Desiree. He poured all of his energies into creating this haven, praying that at the end of the day he would be too damned exhausted to think or feel. Some days his efforts paid off. Many times it did not, and she would creep into his thoughts, beneath his skin.

Lincoln inhaled deeply the salt-filled air and he could almost feel her fill him as she had always done. But he knew how empty he truly was inside. When would the emptiness be filled? He closed his eyes for a moment as the images came rushing back.

The sounds of laughter floated upward from the shore and pulled him from the thoughts that constantly engulfed him. He opened his eyes, turned and slowly walked back to the main house.

"Terri, I'm going into town," Lincoln said as he approached the front desk. "I should be back in an hour or so. Is there anything we need—you need?"

Terri put the guest register aside. "We're pretty well stocked with everything. We had a shipment of supplies on Friday."

Lincoln nodded.

"Are you okay, Mr. D.? You seem so out of it lately."

He chuckled. "Naw, I'm okay. Didn't know it was that obvious."

She tipped her head to the side and smiled. "You're pretty lousy at hiding your feelings, Mr. D."

"Guess I have to work on that." He tapped the desk and walked toward the door. "See you later."

Driving always had a way of relaxing him, he thought, as he trotted down the four steps to the driveway and got behind the wheel of his black-on-black Lincoln Navigator. He had to do something to keep his mind off of Desiree's impending visit. More than once, he'd thought about leaving The Port and staying at his place in Manhattan until he was sure she was gone. But he realized the only purpose it would serve would be to delay the inevitable. He always believed that at some point in life he and Desiree would meet again and be forced to confront their demons. That it would be here and now meant that the time had come.

He took a turn onto the main two-lane road to be met by a speeding car that came right at him. He swerved violently to the right and onto the shoulder to avoid a head-on collision. Squealing to a stop, he looked in his rearview mirror. The tan Volvo continued down the road and turned off onto the same road he'd come from as if nothing nearly disastrous had just occurred.

Lincoln spat out a string of expletives before pulling himself together and getting back onto the road.

"Some people need to have their licenses taken away," he grumbled.

"Idiot!" Rachel yelled.

Desiree held her hand to her chest. "Jeez, Rae. That was close."

"It's obvious that whoever was behind the wheel doesn't practice any road courtesy," she huffed, attempting to hide how shaken she was behind a blast of bravado. She gripped the steering wheel.

"Well, just relax. It can't be too much farther."

Desiree peeked into the passenger-side mirror and watched the magnificent black stallion of a ride disappear as Rachel turned onto the next road. An unsettling sensation floated upward from her belly and gripped her heart. She suddenly felt hot and cold as if something had passed over or through her. Her heart beat a little faster but she was no longer sure if it was a result of their recent scare...or something else. She glanced in the mirror again and saw nothing but road and trees. She took a deep, cleansing breath and pushed the odd feelings aside.

Chapter 6

Rachel pulled up to the main house of The Port, an imposing white structure, reminiscent of mansions in the old South, complete with pillars, a wraparound balcony and an enclosed porch all embraced by towering willows that swayed gently in the light breeze off the water.

"Impressive," Rachel said, easing the car to a stop.

"Very nice." Desiree opened her door and stepped out. She looked around and immediately felt a sense of ease and tranquility move through her.

Terri opened the front door, came out onto the porch and waved. "Welcome to The Port," she said, approaching the duo. "Did you have a good trip?"

"Yes, except for a near mishap on the road," Rachel grumbled.

"Sorry about that. I'm Terri," she said, extending her hand to Rachel and then Desiree.

"Rachel Givens."

"Desiree Armstrong."

"Oh, Ms. Armstrong." Terri smiled. "I know you'll enjoy your stay with us."

"I'm sure I will."

"Leave your bags. I'll have someone come and get them. If you'll follow me, I'll get you all checked in and set you up with your cabin."

They followed her inside. Rachel filled out all the appropriate forms.

"Will you be needing special meals or anything, Ms. Armstrong?"

"No, not at all. I'm easy."

"We have breakfast here in the main house in the dining room from seven to ten. Lunch is on your own. But the fridge is always stocked, so feel free to fix whatever you like. We offer dinner as well, but many of our guests choose to go into town for the evening. So just let me know if you decide to eat in."

"Sounds wonderful." Desiree smiled.

"Okay, well, let me take you to your cabin." She looked toward the door. "Oh, Josh, would you please take Ms. Armstrong's bags to cabin six?"

"Sure."

Terri unlocked the cabin and opened the door. "As you can see, you have all the comforts of home." She opened a door and flipped on the light. "Full-size bath with Jacuzzi." She walked across the room and opened the blinds. "This is one of my favorite cabins. It has the greatest view of the water. You have phone service, a wet bar—on the house—cable television, a business area with a fax machine and a computer should you need to use it." She opened a side door. "This is your sitting room."

The intimate room had a fireplace, sliding glass doors that led to a flowered walkway, a small fabric-covered couch and love seat in a warm brandy color, a smoked-glass coffee table and a twenty-seven-inch television and stereo system.

"Up at the main house we have a masseuse, full gym and heated swimming pool." She took a breath and turned to them with a smile. "Anything you need, just call. I hope it meets with all of your expectations."

"This is incredible," Desiree said, taking in the amenities. "Nothing like any 'cabin' I've ever seen."

Terri laughed. "That's what all of our guests say. Well, I'll let you get settled." She walked to the door. "Should we expect you for dinner?"

"That might be nice. Thank you."

"Great. Dinner is at eight." She closed the door behind her.

"Hey, girl, you hit the jackpot," Rachel said, falling out across the queen-size bed.

"I can't thank you enough. This is fabulous. How did you find it anyway?"

"Trust me, it wasn't easy. It was the last one on the shore that wasn't filled. Apparently it's rather new and wasn't listed."

"I'm glad you did. I'm sure I'm going to love it here."

Rachel looked at her watch. "I hate to run, but I think I should head back." She pulled herself up from the bed and stood.

"Thanks for bringing me up here and for everything." Desiree wrapped her in a hug.

"Anything for you, sis." She kissed Desiree's cheek. "I'll walk you back to the car."

There was a knock on the door. It was Josh with Desiree's bags.

"Where would you like these?" he asked.

"You can put them by the bed." She dug in her purse for a tip and handed him five dollars.

"Thank you." He shoved the money in his pocket. "Will you be needing anything else?"

"No, I'm fine for now."

"Listen, you get settled. I'll walk back with Josh," Rachel said. "If you don't mind, Josh."

"Actually we can ride back. I have a little golf cart out front."

"Perfect. These aren't the best shoes in the world for walking," she said, referring to her designer pumps.

"Well, make sure you call me when you get back to the city. And take it easy on the road," Desiree warned.

"I will. Promise."

Desiree stood at the door and watched them drive

away, then returned to her room. She glanced around and pulled in a deep breath. "Well, let the healing begin," she said softly.

"Hey there, Mr. D.," Terri greeted. "Our guest arrived about an hour ago. I put her in six. She seems really nice."

Lincoln's heart knocked hard in his chest. He cleared his throat. "Good. Uh, is she alone or…"

"She checked in by herself. A friend drove her up. I hope she'll be comfortable here. She seemed a little sad, but maybe it's all in my head."

"Why would you think that? Did she…say anything?"

"No. She didn't say anything in particular. It was in her eyes. You know how I am about reading people. Are you going up to introduce yourself?"

"Maybe a little later. I'm sure she wants to rest." He started to walk away. "I'll be in the back if you need me."

"Sure thing, Mr. D."

Lincoln went out of the main house to the back of the building. He slung his hands into the pockets of his sweatpants and looked across the landscape to where cabin number six stood. He could see movement behind the partially opened vertical blinds. *Desiree.* She was mere feet away from him. All it would take was a short walk, a knock on her door, and they would stand face-to-face.

But it was obvious that she didn't want to see him.

She hadn't asked for his whereabouts. She didn't leave a message at the desk. It was clear to him that even after all this time she still didn't want to see him.

He lowered his head, turned and walked away.

Chapter 7

Desiree finished unpacking her belongings, tried out the remote on the television, tested that the phone was working, fixed herself a glass of rum and Coke, then decided to take a walk outside before the sun set.

She changed from her very stylish but impractical open-toed sandals and put on her black Reeboks, then took her well-worn denim jacket from the hook behind the door and walked outside.

Deciding to be adventurous, she took the path that led away from the main house and opted for the one that wound its way in and out of the property and down to the water.

She took her time, stopping along the way to pick wildflowers and wave to several couples that she passed. It was so peaceful, she mused, and the first time she hadn't felt the constriction in her chest or the constant swirling in the pit of her stomach. She tugged in lungfuls of ocean-washed air as if to force all remnants of that night from her body.

For a moment she closed her eyes and tried to will away the last of her fears. Everything happens for a reason, her grandmother always said, even though the reasons may not be clear, and God never gives you more than you can bear.

Those words, that philosophy, had been a source of consolation and strength to her at some of the lowest points in her life. No, she didn't understand why all that she cared about was taken from her for a second time. She believed that after what happened between her and Lincoln, she could pour all of her love and passion into her work as a way to heal. Now even that was taken from her.

She opened her eyes and looked toward the heavens as tears of anguish and confusion spilled down her cheeks. "Why, God, why?" she cried out.

"I ask myself the same question," came a voice as gentle as the breeze that wafted around her and just as familiar.

For an instant her head spun and her heart raced wildly in an unnatural rhythm. Slowly she turned and the world seemed to stand still.

He was still just as incredibly beautiful as she remembered him in her dreams. His eyes as dark and penetrating, the mouth that had said and done exquisite things to her mind and body were the same. And that unrelenting ache that she had for him in the center of her spirit was still as intense. It wasn't supposed to be like this, she thought. Not after all this time. She wasn't supposed to want to run into his arms and melt in the comfort of his embrace, but damn if she didn't.

The sadness in her eyes was there, Lincoln observed. But she was still as beautiful as he remembered—fragile yet resilient. She made you want to take care of her and rely on her strength at the same time. How many nights had he dreamed of seeing her again, holding her, making love with her? This must be the sign that he'd prayed for. It had to be.

"Lincoln…what are you doing here?"

He dared to step closer. "The place is mine."

She blinked several times as if to get him in focus. "What?"

"The place is mine. I own The Port." He spread his arms expansively. "All of it."

Desiree didn't know whether to be angry or to laugh at the twisted reality of it all. *Did Rachel intentionally bring her here, knowing that Lincoln owned the resort?* she wondered, the nagging thought jumping into her head.

"That's really nice for you," she said, her voice tight. "Seems like you're doing well for yourself."

"It's what we talked about. Remember?"

Her heart lurched then settled. She folded her arms as if that could somehow contain her emotions.

"I remember a lot of things."

"So do I, Des. Not all of them bad."

She turned her back to him, unable to look at the past that was mirrored in his eyes.

"I came out here to be alone. If you don't mind." Her voice was as sharp and cold as an axe.

Lincoln straightened his shoulders. "I've never stopped loving you, Desiree. I'll leave you with that."

A wave of emotion welled within her, heating her body, causing her veins to throb in her temples. She didn't want to love him, not ever again. Each night she prayed that her feelings for him would disappear so that she could live again. But that prayer had not been answered.

She turned around and he was gone and for a moment she believed it was only one of her dreams—an apparition. But she knew it was neither. She felt his presence surround her as surely as if he'd held her all through the night.

"Lincoln," she whispered.

Desiree glanced toward the main house. Her immediate thought was to return to her cabin, pack her bags and find a way back to Manhattan. But that would be the easy way, the cowardly way. The only thing she'd ever walked away from in her life had been her relationship with Lincoln, and she promised herself, standing in that space, that she wouldn't do it again.

* * *

Lincoln returned to the main house—shaken. He had no idea what the impact of seeing Desiree again would be like. He'd imagined it hundreds of times, but the reality was something completely different.

The raw hurt and anger was still in her eyes, in the stiffness of her shoulders, the chill of her words. Like a fool he'd romanticized their meeting. In his mind's eye he saw them shedding the past, sharing words of forgiveness and ultimately finding their way back into each other's lives.

It was obvious that was not to be. Then why was she here? To pour salt in his still-open wounds? To prove to him that she still didn't need or want him in her life as she'd said that night?

Maybe it was best that he leave until she was gone, he thought as he opened the front door.

"We have a problem, Mr. D.," Terri said, the instant he crossed the threshold.

"What is it?"

She handed him a printout.

He looked over the figures and frowned. "Did you notify Ms. Armstrong?" he asked a bit too quickly.

"No. I thought I should speak to you first. When her friend Rachel Givens made all of the arrangements she was so insistent that she was going to take care of everything and that Ms. Armstrong was not to be bothered." She pursed her lips and folded her arms. "So what do we do?"

Lincoln stuck the printout in his back pants pocket. "Wait a day or two and try to put the costs through again. If there is still a problem, let me know."

"Okay," she said, making the word three syllables.

"I'll be in the back office."

He walked off and shut the door behind him, pulling the paper from his pocket as he crossed the room to his desk. He sat down in the swivel chair, a treat to himself when he'd closed on the property. He spun the chair to face the window, and gazed out onto the cabins beyond. What were Desiree and Rachel trying to pull?

Chapter 8

"What?"

"You heard me, Rae. Lincoln owns this place lock, stock and barrel!" She pressed her fingers to her temple in an attempt to massage away the throbbing that was building by degrees.

"Desi, I swear, I had no idea."

Desiree grumbled something unintelligible. "I know how much you've been lobbying for me and Lincoln to get back together, but this!"

"Desiree Armstrong, I know good and well you don't think I set this up."

Desiree squeezed her eyes shut for a moment and sighed. "I don't know what to think at the moment. Every limb is shaking and my brain is on scramble."

"Look, if you want to leave I'll come up and get you."

Desiree was silent.

"Well, do you?"

"No," she snapped. "I'm not going to let him run me off."

Rachel breathed a sigh of relief. "Well…maybe it's for the best, you know."

"No, I don't know," she snapped and rolled her eyes at no one in particular. "But like Grandma always said, everything happens for a reason."

"The reason is pretty clear to me."

"Oh, really? And what might that be?"

"You two were destined to meet again. Let's be real. What are the odds that you would want to come to Sag Harbor and the only available place to stay is owned by your ex-fiancé? That's the kinda stuff that only happens in books and made-for-TV movies."

Desiree had to chuckle despite herself. "Yeah, I guess you're right. It is kind of freaky."

"For real."

They were thoughtful for a moment.

"So, what are you going to do, girl? You can't stay holed up in your room. You're bound to run into him again."

"I know. I suppose I'll deal with it…some kind of way."

"Desi…I know the subject of you and Lincoln has

been off-limits. But just between us, do you still, you know…still care about him?"

"I've never stopped caring about him," she quietly confessed, then stretched out on the bed. She crossed her bare ankles. "I think about Lincoln almost every waking hour of my days. I dream of him at night. I hear his voice in my head."

"So why, Des? Why have you stayed away? Why won't you tell him how you feel?"

Desiree swallowed over the knot in her throat as the old pain rose from her belly.

"Because…" Her voice cracked like fine china falling to the floor. "I don't ever want to love and lose like that again."

"Well, where is she?" Carl demanded.

Cynthia blocked the entrance to her apartment door. She placed one hand on her hip.

"I don't know where she is," she said, enunciating every word.

Carl adjusted his navy silk tie and clenched his teeth. "I don't believe you." He pointed his index finger in her face. "You know where she is and I want you to tell me!"

"If you don't leave now I'm calling the police."

Carl opened his mouth to say something but stopped, then abruptly turned and left.

Cynthia slammed the door and went straight for the phone. She dialed the operator.

"Yes, could I please have the number for Honey

Child Accessories?" She took a pencil from the desk drawer, listened to the recorded voice and jotted down the number on a paper napkin. She hung up and dialed the number.

"Thank you for calling Honey Child…"

Cynthia listened and waited to leave her message after the tone. For several moments she sat there staring into space.

Carl got into his Mercedes and tore away from the curb. Cynthia was lying, he inwardly fumed. There had to be a way to find out where Desiree was. She couldn't have vanished into thin air.

Why would she leave without saying a word? She owed him. He knew he should have gone to see her in the hospital. But he called every day to check on her progress and then one day he was told she was gone. He should have forced himself to cross the hospital's threshold, but he had a phobia about hospitals ever since he was eight years old and his mother forced him to visit his sick grandmother.

She had tubes everywhere, he recalled, and monitors that beeped eerily in the stark white room. She looked like a ghost beneath the stiff sheets. Her chest barely rose and fell and he could almost hear the drip, drip of the clear fluid that coursed through the plastic tubes into the thin blue veins that stood out against her parchment-like skin.

"Go on, Carl," his mother urged in a hushed hospital whisper. "Say hello to your grandma." She pushed him forward and he stumbled against the metal frame of the bed and suddenly his grandmother opened her eyes. They were black and sunken in her head. The rims were bloodred and watery. She reached out and grabbed his hand with fingers that felt like slivers of ice. Carl screamed and ran from the room. From that day to this he'd never set foot in another hospital room.

He came to a stop at the light. He'd done everything he could to show Desiree that he cared. And now all that he'd done for her had literally gone up in smoke. This was not part of the plan. He had accountants and lawyers breathing down his neck, not to mention investors. He had commitments to fulfill. He didn't even know if he should proceed with the opening in the fall—if she was even able to work.

He had passed what was left of the loft and gallery. Whatever wasn't destroyed by fire and water, the firefighters took care of.

The blaring car horn behind him jerked him from his marauding thoughts. He gave the driver the bird and sped through the intersection.

He had to find her. He had to make her come back. Too much was riding on it. He'd been a fool to let his emotions outweigh his reason. But one thing he was certain of, he didn't play to lose. He would find Desiree, get her back where she belonged and the exhibit would go on as planned.

Carl eased the car to a stop in front of his co-op apartment on the Upper East Side of Manhattan. As usual, the neighborhood was quiet. The few people on the street were out walking their designer dogs or jogging in their designer workout attire. The cars glided down the smooth, black-tarred road. A few lights twinkled in the windows, showcasing cathedral ceilings, lavish dining rooms and beautiful people.

This was his world. Sterile and unimaginative.

With great reluctance he got out of his car and walked toward his building. Had he not met Desiree he would have been content with this life of illusion. But Desiree put color into his otherwise bland existence.

He turned the key in the lock and entered his empty apartment, wishing that Desiree was on the other side waiting for him.

Chapter 9

Desiree hung up from her conversation with Rachel and couldn't help but conclude that her dear friend was just a bit too happy about her present circumstance.

But what Desiree felt like doing was throwing something. How could fate be so cruel? She got up from the bed and stomped off to the bathroom. Maybe a hot bath would help to unfurl her nerves.

With the sudsy, scented water as hot as she could stand it, she eased her body in and slid down until the bubbles reached her chin, then leaned back and closed her eyes.

Perhaps she dozed off, but as surely as if she'd summoned him from the depths of the slightly rippling water, Lincoln appeared before her, gloriously naked, stroking the tender inside of her thighs.

Desiree adjusted herself in the tub to give him more room, better access to the throb that beat relentlessly within her.

His fingers played with her warm flesh, raising the hairs on her arms as his fingers trailed along her hips, the slight swell of her stomach, up to her nipples that rose to delicate peaks above the water. Involuntarily she moaned when he took one into his mouth, taunting it with wicked flicks of his tongue.

"Desi…"

His voice was like music, the deepest bass, vibrating through her like an echo. She trembled.

"Lincoln…"

Tears of longing slipped from behind her closed lids. "I still love you, too."

A pounding in the distance drew her from the grip of her erotic fantasy. She opened her eyes, bringing the room back into focus, though the remnants of her illusion lingered. The knocking came again. Reluctantly she pulled herself out of the water, took the hotel's terry cloth robe from the hook behind the bathroom door and wrapped it around her dripping body.

No one knew she was there, so she certainly wasn't expecting company, she thought, wiping her eyes as she walked into the front room. It must be someone from the main house. "They could have called," she grumbled, willing her body to relinquish its grip on her daydream.

She tightened the belt on the robe, swiped a damp lock off her forehead and pulled open the door.

"You didn't come up for dinner, and I thought you might be hungry."

Her heart raced so fast she could barely breathe. She swallowed hard.

"I…" She pulled the robe closer together. "Thank you."

Lincoln handed her the covered tray.

"Smells good," she murmured, desperately trying to avoid his pointed stare.

So do you. "I only hire the best," he said, instead of what he thought.

"Um…do you want to come in for a minute?"

He hesitated.

"Maybe another time. I don't want to intrude. You did say you wanted to be alone. I'll respect that."

She glanced down at her damp, bare feet, then up at him.

"I…I'd like that. The some other time." A faint smile lifted the corners of her mouth.

Lincoln smiled and nodded his head, but what he wanted to do was reach out and touch her, feel her beneath the pads of his fingers. He wanted to hold her against him and inhale the freshly washed scent of her. His loins ached with denial, and he knew if he didn't leave right then…

"Whenever you're ready, Desi, I'm here."

She tugged in a shaky breath. "Thanks. I'll remember that."

"Good night."

"Night," she whispered and watched him walk away.

Mindlessly she closed the door with her foot, turned, put the tray on the center of the bed and realized she was shaking like a leaf.

"Get over it, girl," she said aloud.

She wrapped her arms around her body to still the tremors.

He'd been so close. Just the two of them in her bedroom. All she would have to do was ask him to come in one more time and she knew he would have given in. She saw it in his eyes, the way he slowly licked his lips, the way he used to when he was about to say yes to her.

But then what? she thought. They would have tumbled into bed together, clawed at each other's clothes and made crazy love until the sun rose over the water. Yeah, that's what would have happened if she'd pressed a little harder.

She kicked at her suitcase with her bare foot.

"Idiot!" she hissed.

Lincoln paced the floor of his suite like a panther in heat. He slung his hands into his pockets, then took them out. He walked to the window and pulled back the curtains. If he stared really hard he could almost see

Desiree walking through her room in front of the open sliding doors with the breeze from the ocean blowing through her sheer gown.

He squeezed his eyes shut and raked his fingers through his close-cropped hair. Groaning low in his throat, he pulled the door open and stormed out.

Desiree sat on the side of the bed nibbling at the grilled salmon, wild rice and Caesar salad. The food was delicious, just as Lincoln had boasted. He always did things in style and it was true that he never settled for less than the best. This place and everything about Lincoln Davenport echoed that fact.

From the day they had met eight years earlier on the corner of 34th Street and 8th Avenue in the middle of a snowstorm, two days before Christmas, she knew he was something special...

"Looks like you're trying to do the same thing I am."

Desiree had looked up, trying to focus on the tall dark figure in front of her with the snow swirling around them.

"Huh?" she shouted over a gust of wind that seemed to carry her voice in the opposite direction. She shielded her eyes by cupping her hand above her brow.

"Trying to catch a cab," the man shouted.

Desiree nodded her head and hunched her shoulders to keep the snow from sliding down her neck. She could kick herself for forgetting her scarf. But the weatherman said a "chance" of flurries, not a full-blown snowstorm. Ha! What did they know with all their fancy equipment? It had been snowing nonstop for a little more than two hours, building in momentum, and now you could hardly see five feet in front of you.

"I'm heading downtown. Maybe we could share one—if you're going that way."

Desiree tried to get a good look at him. He didn't look like a stalker, but in this weather who could tell?

"So am I," she said.

"Great."

Pedestrians slipped and slid around her, dashing for cover and jostling each other on the snow-covered streets. One woman lost her footing and slid into Desiree, knocking her and her shopping bag to the ground.

"Oh…oh. I'm so sorry," the woman muttered, but didn't hang around long enough to be of any help.

It took a moment for Desiree to register what had happened. One minute she was standing and the next she was sitting on her behind in a pile of snow.

A pair of strong hands slid beneath her arms and lifted her to her feet.

"Are you okay?" he asked as he reached for her shopping bag.

"Yes. I think so," she said, suddenly embarrassed. She brushed the wet snow from her coat. "Thank you."

"Maybe you need to hold on to something," he said, a light chuckle in his deep voice. He took her hand and hooked it in the crook of his arm, drawing her close to the warmth of his body. He patted her leather-covered hand. "I wouldn't want to see you get knocked over by another senior citizen."

She looked up at him and he was smiling. The corners of his mouth were lifted to a perfect angle, revealing just a hint of even, pearly white teeth. His eyes crinkled at the corners and seemed to sparkle with a boyish mischief that made her stomach suddenly quiver. It was the sexiest smile she'd ever seen.

He stuck out his arm and like a magician made a cab appear.

"Come on." He opened the door and helped her inside before easing in next to her.

"Where to?" the cabbie asked, inching away from the curb.

The windshield wipers licked furiously against the driving snow, offering only split seconds of visibility.

Desiree turned to her knight in black cashmere. "I'm going to 22nd Street and 7th Avenue."

"Really? There's a building that I'm looking to buy over there." He settled back in the cab and dusted the snow from his coat.

"You're buying a building?" she asked incredulously. The only people she knew who bought whole buildings were in the newspapers and on TV dramas.

"You sound surprised or skeptical. I can't tell."

He grinned, and this time Mother Nature didn't stand between her and that smile. Her heart lurched in her chest.

Desiree dipped her head for a moment. "I wouldn't say skeptical, maybe surprised."

He folded his hands on his lap. "Tell me why."

His gaze was so direct and penetrating that she imagined he could read her thoughts as easily as strip her naked with only a simple look.

Desiree swallowed and blinked away the vision. "It's just that I don't know many—well, any—black folks who own buildings other than their homes."

"That's one of the best-kept secrets," he joked.

"I know I must sound naive, but…"

"Not at all. Like I said, it's a pretty common belief. But the truth is, there are hundreds of black real estate owners."

"So what do you do with these buildings?" she asked, genuinely interested.

"Some of them I rehab and sell. Others I keep."

"How many do you have?"

"Six."

Her eyes widened. "A regular Donald Trump."

He laughed. "I have a long way to go. By the way, my name is Lincoln Davenport."

"Desiree Armstrong."

He stuck out his hand and Desiree placed hers in it, and when his fingers closed around hers a flood of heat shot through her like a good brandy.

"Pleasure," he uttered.

The deep vibration of his voice sent a shiver up

her spine and it had nothing to do with the bone-numbing cold.

"So what do you do?"

"I paint."

"For a living?"

She giggled. "If that's what you want to call it. But my teaching is what actually pays the bills."

"Ah, the starving artist in person. So tell me, why do you paint?"

For a moment she was taken aback. She'd never been asked why she painted, only what.

She took a breath and turned to him. "For as long as I can remember, there were images running around in my head. I could see things in the ordinary that others couldn't. And the images and colors nag at me, compel me to bring them to life. When I paint or sculpt, it's as if I'm transported, driven. It fuels me with energy, an ongoing passion. I...don't know what I would do if I couldn't create."

"Wow. I'm sold."

She lowered her head, embarrassed for gushing like a schoolgirl. "I must sound like an idealistic nut."

"No, you sound like someone who truly loves what she does. That's rare."

Suddenly the cab swerved to the right, tossing Desiree against Lincoln's hard chest.

Instinctively he grabbed her. "We've got to stop meeting like this," he said with that wicked sparkle in his eyes.

Her breath skidded in her chest as she realized her mouth was inches away from his.

"Sorry about that, folks," the cabbie said, breaking the magic spell in concert with a knock on the door.

Desiree shook her head, and that snowy afternoon was replaced by warmth and green.

"Just a moment." She went to the door and opened it.

"I know I shouldn't be here…"

She took his hand. "Come in, Lincoln."

Chapter 10

Rachel took her glass of white wine and went into her home office to check her messages. She was expecting an overseas call from one of her jewelry suppliers, and the call was already two days late. Any further delay with this shipment was going to cause her major problems with her clients. She'd make sure never to use this supplier again.

She set her wineglass down on the desk and depressed her messages-waiting button.

"This better be you, Javier," she muttered.

The last person she expected to hear from was Cynthia. She frowned as she listened to the message.

Damn. Well, if she had anything to do with it, Carl wouldn't get anywhere near Desiree. The last thing she needed now was to be hassled by Carl. Rachel could never understand how Desiree allowed herself to get so deeply involved with him anyway.

She knew part of it was Desiree's determination to make it in the art world despite her breakup with Lincoln. It was her way of showing him that she could survive without him, and also of putting her pain behind her. But she hadn't succeeded on either score. Not really. She'd merely existed through her work. Now she didn't even have that.

Rachel took a sip of her wine. But now that opportunity had stepped in and brought them back together, maybe Desiree would finally come to her senses and put the past behind her for good and move into the future—with Lincoln.

Rachel picked up the phone and called Cynthia.

"Have a seat," Desiree said as she shut the door.

Lincoln stepped in and turned to her.

"Desi, we really need to talk."

"I know," she said softly.

She crossed the room and sat at the foot of the bed.

"I don't want you to be uncomfortable staying here. If my presence bothers you I'll leave until you check out."

"You don't need to do that."

He took a breath and asked the question that had been nagging at him.

"Why did you decide to come here of all places?"

"To be truthful, it wasn't my choice." She paused.

"Rachel found it. I had no idea this was your place and neither did she. Although for a minute there I swore she did. You know Rachel," she said not unkindly.

They chuckled with the knowledge of Rachel's true feelings about their breakup and her one-woman campaign to get them back together.

Lincoln traced and retraced his steps across the floor before finally sitting down. He braced his forearms on his hard thighs and leaned slightly forward.

"How have you been, Desi?" he asked with genuine concern. "I mean, really." His eyes probed hers.

"Getting better," she said on a whispered breath. She looked away.

"What do you mean…getting better?"

Desiree inhaled deeply and straightened her shoulders, then slowly told him what had happened, at least parts of it. She left out the part about her losing everything, that she was still afraid to go to sleep, that she couldn't paint, that all she had left in the world was a meager savings account and her car and that she owed Carl Hampton thousands of dollars.

"Oh, Des…I…I'm so sorry. I didn't know."

She lowered her head to hide the tears and the pain that lingered in her eyes.

Lincoln got up and sat beside her. With caution, he put his arm around her, drawing her head to rest on his shoulder.

"It's okay, baby. It's okay," he murmured. "You're still here. That's the only thing that matters. God…

if I had lost you," he uttered in a strangled voice and pulled her closer, stroking the wiry twists of her hair. He closed his eyes and inhaled the scent of her. He couldn't imagine the possibility of never seeing her again.

"What are your plans? You know you can stay here as long as you want," he offered.

"Thanks." She sniffed hard and eased out of his embrace. "I'm sorry." She wiped her eyes. "There was no reason to put all of that on you." She shook her head. "It's not your concern."

Abruptly he stood and looked down at her lowered head. "Not my concern? Isn't that where our problems started, when you decided that things that affected both of us weren't my concern?" His voice shook from the years of holding back, of waiting for this moment of confrontation. "Did you honestly believe that what was happening to you had nothing to do with me?" He paced, then shot back at her, "I lost our baby, too. Did you ever once think about how I felt?"

They stared at each other, neither willing to back down or find a middle ground.

Desiree stood, her mouth set in a firm line of defiance. She walked right up to him.

"You have no idea what it feels like to have a life growing inside of you," she said, speaking in measured beats. "And then in the blink of an eye, it's gone and all your chances for another…" Her voice broke. Her nostrils flared as she sucked in air, willing herself not to cry again.

"Desiree." He reached for her.

"Don't." She held up her hands. "I don't want your sympathy, Lincoln." She turned away.

"Sympathy? Is that really what you think?" he asked, totally stunned.

"I don't need you to feel sorry for me, my 'situation.'" She raised her chin. "I've been doing perfectly fine by myself."

"I see." The corners of his mouth dipped in disappointment. He walked toward the door and opened it. "The offer to stay as long as you need still stands," he said, his voice barely above a whisper. "I won't bother you again. I was a fool to think… Goodbye, Desiree."

The next sound she heard was the door rattling in its hinges. She turned toward it, her eyes resolute and her soul empty. "How could I ever tell you that I'm no longer a real woman?" she whispered.

Slowly she turned back around and took in her space. Maybe she should go back home. *Home*. What a joke. She walked through the cabin and out the sliding door that led to the back.

He would never understand, she reasoned, taking a seat on a high, flat rock while she watched the water trickle between the intricate pathways of the garden. He had no idea the kind of pressure and expectations that were put on her by her oversized, in-your-face family— the main reason why she moved from the family enclave in Charlotte, North Carolina, to attend school in D.C. After graduation she kept going, straight to New York.

Her immediate family was the size of a small town and that did not include the tribe of extended aunts, uncles and cousins through marriage or otherwise. The Armstrong family reunions made the *Charlotte Times* every year as one of the biggest events of the season. And every year she'd be grilled by her mother, grandmother, two sisters and maternal aunts about when she was going to settle down with a good man and have some babies.

"When I'm ready," she'd say, stirring the pot of seasoned collard greens. She'd drop in pieces of smoked turkey for some added flavor.

"Well, you need to hurry up and get ready," her aunt Mae, her mother's oldest sister would say. "In a minute all your good years will be behind you."

"A woman needs to have a family of her own to feel like a real woman," her mother would say.

"Amen." This from Aunt Pearl, the youngest of the trio of sisters. "Children are the glue that holds a man and woman together."

"That may have been true when you and Ma were coming up, Aunt Pearl, but women have so many more options now," Desiree would say in her own defense.

"I have no desire to try to make it in a man's world," her sister Kim would say, rubbing her hand across her eight-month, protruding belly. "Kevin loves taking care of me and the kids and I love letting him."

"There's nothing to compare to being a mother," Denise, Desiree's baby sister, would say. "You feel complete, full of a kind of power that is indescribable. Women bring life into the world. You can't get any better than that. Even men for all their bravado are brought to their knees when their wife has a baby."

"Go forth and multiply is what the Good Book says," her mother would add.

Up against that kind of relentless firepower, Desiree didn't stand a chance. And after… She could never bring herself to tell her family about the doctor's dire prognosis. She didn't want their pity or to hear any old wives' tales about barren women.

She'd never told anyone, not even Rachel, what the doctors told her during her follow-up visit. It was too painful, too humiliating.

Lincoln deserved a woman who could have children, someone he could have a family with. She loved him enough to let him go. And that's what she'd done. Stepped out of his life so that he could find someone else, even though it was slowly killing her inside.

She was a fool to think that even for a minute there could ever be anything between them again. She'd let her emotions and her fantasies and her smoldering desire for him cloud her reason.

It wouldn't happen again. At least that was her plan. But as her favorite R&B crooner, Luther Vandross, sang... *if only for one night.*

Chapter 11

"I'm going into the city," Lincoln announced the following morning.

"Everything is under control, so take your time," Terri said. "We have a guest arriving later this afternoon, but that's about it."

"Fine." He turned to leave. "You can reach me on my cell if anything urgent comes up," he tossed over his shoulder.

"Are you okay, Mr. D.? You look a little tired around your eyes."

"Rough night, but I'll be fine. See you later."

Lincoln strode out, hopped into his Navigator, gunned the engine and took off. He put on a pair of dark shades to dim the glare from the sun that bounced off the water. It was an incredible day, he thought absently. A day that brought visitors from all over to Sag Harbor.

Historically, Sag Harbor was one of the original enclaves for free blacks who had never been slaves. This group, the black whalers and their families, European immigrants, Native Americans and other people of color thrived in Sag Harbor, living in Eastville. In the early 1900s African-Americans began to summer in Sag Harbor, and it was at that point that many black professionals began to move there, their descendants continuing to live and own property there. At that time blacks were restricted to the waterfront because it was deemed less desirable. Today, homes on the beachfront property often sold in excess of a million dollars. Talk about irony.

It was one of the main reasons why Lincoln chose to buy there. Although he was not part of the community's rich past, he wanted to ensure that he would be part of its future.

The beauty, the history, the inhabitants, none of it mattered. Not today. All he wanted to do was put some distance between him and Desiree.

How could she have grown so cold? She was not the woman he remembered, although there were moments when the old spark of love and passion was reflected in her eyes. But her tone was as chilling as an arctic blast.

Didn't she realize that she wasn't the only one who was hurt, who suffered? Instead of them dealing with it together, she'd turned on him as if he'd become the enemy. She'd refused to listen to reason, and one night when he'd come in from work all that she'd left behind in their one-bedroom apartment was her scent and a note.

All his attempts to reach her failed. He even went to Pratt Institute where she taught art appreciation classes, and he wasn't allowed past security.

He'd been so angry during those days. Some nights he would prowl the streets of New York City until sunrise. Other nights he would visit the local bar and drink until Stewart, the bartender, had to send him home in a cab or take him home himself.

"Whatever or whoever has your head all screwed up isn't worth killing yourself over," Stewart had warned one rainy September night.

"Just keep filling my glass with the Jack Daniel's and we can stay friends," Lincoln slurred, trying to merge the two Stewarts into one.

"I think you've had more than enough for tonight." He took away Lincoln's glass and wiped down the space in front of him with a damp off-white towel. "You just chill for a few and I'll drive you home after I lock up."

"That will be necessary," Lincoln mumbled.

Stewart smirked and shook his head. "Who is she?" he asked.

Lincoln looked up at him through bleary eyes.

"She was gonna by my wife," he muttered. "We had plans, but she left me."

"Did she have a reason?"

"Said…she didn't love me anymore. Just like that." He tried unsuccessfully to snap his fingers. "But she's lying. She has to be lying. 'Cause I know I still love her, so she's gotta still love me, too. Ya know?"

"Give it some time. Maybe she's just running scared."

"You really think so, man?" he asked, the first spark of hope in his voice.

"Yeah, just give it some time."

And that's what he'd done. It had been five long years and his feelings were as strong for Desiree now as they were then. Every day he'd wake up and hope that the ache would be gone, but it wasn't. He'd tried to bury his loneliness and his hurt in the bodies of other women over the years, but it didn't help. If anything it only made him realize that no one would be able to take her place in his heart.

Finally, he'd resigned himself to being alone or at least not in a committed relationship—and then she turned up on his doorstep.

He knew he couldn't spend the rest of his life in this emotionless limbo. What he needed was closure. He needed answers. He hoped to find them in New York.

Rachel just finished bawling out Javier when the front door to Honey Child opened. Good home training kept her from doing a double take and letting her mouth drop open. She put on her best smile.

"Felicia, finish up with this order," she said to her new assistant, while keeping her eye on her unexpected visitor. "Lincoln." She came from behind the front desk with her hands extended.

He took them and kissed her cheek. "Looking good as always, Rachel."

She blushed. "Always the charmer," she volleyed.

"Is there someplace where we can talk?"

"Sure." She turned to Felicia. "I'll be in the back." She led Lincoln into her small, cluttered office and shut the door. "Please, have a seat."

Lincoln sat on the edge of a wing chair and crossed his right ankle over his left thigh. "I'm not going to waste your time or mine with a lot of idle chatter. I know you set Desiree up at The Port, but why is she really there?"

For a moment she frowned in confusion. "You don't know, do you?"

"Know what?"

"She lost everything in the fire."

"I gathered as much. But that still doesn't explain why she came to Sag Harbor."

She went on to tell him about her stay in the hospital and how depressed and lethargic she'd been. "Desiree has a show that she's contracted for coming up in late September. Her very first one. But with everything gone and Desi unable or unwilling to work…" Her sentence trailed off. "I just thought that a major change in atmosphere and environment would help her."

He shook his head. "Still, after all this time, she wouldn't come to me except by mistake." He looked at Rachel. "I'm glad she has you as a friend. Fate is something else," he added wryly. "Tragedy separated us and now it's brought us back together."

Rachel arched a brow. "Very true." She paused. "So now that you know all of it, what are you going to do?"

"There's not much I can do if Desiree won't let me."

Rachel looked him square in the eye. "Do you still love her?"

"Always."

"Then there's plenty you can do. Desi is stubborn and single-minded. But," her tone softened, "I know she still loves you, Lincoln, although she won't admit it to you. She's just too afraid to say it. And you know she won't let on that she's afraid of anything."

"I've been down that road with her before. She doesn't want to have anything to do with me."

"So she says. I know better and so do you." She smiled. "The trick is convincing her of that."

They talked some more and they agreed to keep each other posted.

"If she ever finds out we are in cahoots, she'd strangle us both," Rachel said.

Lincoln chuckled. "Don't I know it?" He checked his watch. "Well, I guess I'll be heading back. Thanks for talking to me."

"I would have a long time ago if I'd known where to find you."

"Well, you do now." He smiled. "Don't be a stranger."

"I won't." She came from behind her desk. "I'll walk you out. Speaking of finding people, how did you find me?"

"Your credit card information." He got to the front door. "By the way, your card didn't clear," he whispered.

For an instant she looked perplexed, then mortified. "I'll take care of it. I am so sorry. I must have used the wrong card."

"Don't worry about it. Between you and me, Desi's stay is on the house."

"Lincoln, you don't—"

"I want to and it's settled. I can be stubborn, too." He kissed her cheek. "I'll be in touch."

Rachel watched him from the doorway until his vehicle was out of sight, which she now recognized as the one she nearly ran off the road. Fate. Thoughtfully, she closed the door. She'd intentionally left out any information about Carl, and she wondered how long it would take the very resourceful Lincoln Davenport to find out about him.

Chapter 12

By the time Lincoln returned to The Port the sun was beginning to set over the water, tossing brilliant ripples of orange and gold light. A warm breeze blew off the ocean, teasing the profusion of trees that surrounded the property. From his open window he inhaled the pungent scent of salt water, rich dark earth and lush green.

He could see from the road several of his guests departing from the main house to take strolls, return to their cabins, or perhaps go into town for a late movie or an early drink.

On many nights like these he and Desiree used to lie naked in bed, holding hands and whispering to each other their dreams for the future.

"I know that one way to financial security is to own land," Lincoln had said. "I want to replicate what many blacks did in Sag Harbor, buy cheap, improve it and reap the benefits of the escalating market value."

"But what would you build on the beach?" she'd asked, caressing his chest.

He was thoughtful for a moment. "Hmm, a bed-and-breakfast."

She propped herself up on her elbow. "Really?"

"Yep. But not your ordinary B and B, but something that is truly classy and still has that homey feel to it. I think it would be great." He turned on his side. "And we could run it together. We'd have the best facilities, secluded, a great chef, a picture-perfect landscape. Someplace we could call a second home."

Desiree turned on her back and looked up at the ceiling, envisioning his dream in her mind. "Yeah," she said slowly. "I think it could really work."

"It's definitely an idea. I know I don't want to live in the city forever," he added. "The city is a tough town for old folks."

Desiree playfully popped him on the arm. "We have a long way to go before we're old folks," she said with laughter in her voice.

"In some societies you'd be considered an old maid."

She sprang up and leaned over him, looking down into his eyes. "Oh, really?" she said with a hint of challenge in her voice. "Can an old maid do this?"

She ran her tongue provocatively across his lips

while her slender fingers taunted the fine hairs on his chest, then down to the tautness of his belly.

Her lips trailed down to his neck and she took tiny nibbles that caused him to moan softly. She explored the expanse of his chest, flicking one nipple with her tongue and then the next.

Lincoln groaned low in his throat when her butter-soft fingers began to stroke his sex until it rose and hardened in her grasp.

"You're a very naughty old lady," he murmured, pulling her atop him to straddle his body.

She drew up her knees and rose to position herself above his throbbing penis. She gazed down into his eyes.

"Do old ladies feel anything like this?"

She took him inside her by slow, infinitesimal degrees that seemed to go on for an eternity, and he swore he'd explode with longing if he couldn't feel all of her—now. Her sexy torture continued until he could no longer stand it. He grasped her hips and pulled her completely down until the hot, wet walls totally encased him.

Desiree let out a gasp that was a mixture of ecstasy and primal lust.

"Yesss," she hissed through her teeth, tossing her head back and rotating her hips in total abandon.

The soft music from the stereo that played in the background seemed to rise in concert with the tempo that the lovers built.

They whispered sweet, naughty, erotic, challenging words in each other's ears. It was wild. It was wicked. It was how they always were with each other, giving all that they had to give to each other until they lay spent, breathless and totally satisfied.

"Not bad for two old coots," Desiree whispered against Lincoln's still-racing heart.

"This is only the beginning, babe." He gently brushed her damp hair away from her face. "We have a whole lifetime to love each other."

A whole lifetime...

"I was wondering how long you were going to sit there with the engine running."

Lincoln jerked in his seat and blinked back the images, realizing that he'd come to a stop in front of Desiree's cabin.

Desi always had a youthful appearance, but with the softness of the waning light and the revealing outfit of a white tank top, matching shorts and sneakers, she could easily pass for a twenty-year-old. She sported a navy blue baseball cap with the beak pulled down low over her eyes.

"I was just driving around checking on things," he lied smoothly.

"Really?" she asked with a raised left brow. She could always tell when Lincoln was lying. He tugged on his bottom lip just like he was doing now. She folded her arms, deciding not to pursue it. "Beautiful night."

"Yeah, it is. Wanna go for a drive along the beach?"

The words were out before he could catch them and he regretted them the moment he did, certain that his offer would be shot down.

A slow smile moved gently across her full, glossy mouth. "That sounds like a nice idea," she said, surprising them both.

He swallowed and quickly counted trucks in his head to beat back the remnants of his brief sexual odyssey before getting out of the Navigator to open the passenger door for her.

The fullness of her unbound breasts inadvertently brushed his bare arm as she went past him to get in. Simultaneously their gazes locked as that jolt of sensual electricity snapped between them. For a moment, neither moved.

Desiree saw the old flames burning in his eyes and wondered if he could see it in hers as well.

She could have stayed inside the safety of her cabin when she heard his vehicle pull up and come to a stop. She could have stepped outside to investigate in something less revealing. She'd done neither.

Since she'd coldly sent him on his way earlier, she'd had enough time to think, a least a little bit. Who was she fooling? She still loved the man, and he'd said as much to her. The question that remained was, could her heart risk being "in love" with Lincoln again? Did she dare take that chance? The conclusion she reached as she sat on the rocks behind her cabin was that she would never know if she kept running and hiding.

"Thanks," she whispered, breaking the spell and stepping up into the Navigator.

Lincoln tugged in a deep breath, as the luscious scent of her drifted to him, then shut her door and got in behind the wheel.

"So…how did you spend the rest of your day?" Lincoln asked after driving for a few minutes in silence.

"I spent it thinking, actually."

"You want to talk about it?"

She hesitated, debating about changing the subject, then decided to tell him the truth.

"About us…mostly. Me, my life and what I'm going to do with it now."

He briefly glanced in her direction. "I don't know what to ask first. But to be truthful I want to hear about you."

"You always did know how to flatter a girl." She smiled. She tugged in a breath and slowly let it out as if the air she expelled would somehow provide the pathway for the words to follow.

"A lot has happened since…" She stole a look at him and nervously laced and unlaced her fingers. "Since you and me." She saw him flinch ever so slightly. "When I left I moved into a small studio in the West Village…"

She told him about meeting Carl during an art exhibit in SoHo, how they'd talked for hours about art and she'd finally agreed to show him some of her work several weeks later. He was completely enthusiastic about her work and encouraged her to pursue her craft and her passion to paint professionally. She'd explained that she couldn't afford to be a "professional artist," she had bills to pay and a strong desire for three meals a day.

She didn't see Carl for several weeks after that until one day she got a call from him asking to meet him for dinner. Over a glass of wine, he laid out his proposition.

"If there's one thing I can always spot, it's talent," he said, slicing into his medium-rare sirloin. "And if there's one thing I love, it's art. Now combine art and talent and you have an incredible combination. You have both, Desiree."

"Thank you. I—"

He held up his steak knife. "I'm not saying this to flatter you. It's the truth and I want to see you flourish as an artist. I know in my gut that you have what it takes to make it. All you need is money and opportunity."

"Neither of which I have." She lifted her beveled water glass and took a soothing gulp while she wondered where the conversation was going.

"That's where you're wrong."

He went on to tell her how he was willing to finance her pursuit, set her up with a working/living loft with space below for a small gallery where she could sell her work and which she would be totally responsible for running. She could paint, and when she built a sufficient body of work, he would sponsor her very first solo exhibit—every artist's dream.

She'd been stunned into silence. A full-fledged sponsor? She was flattered, frightened, but undeniably excited at the possibility. Teaching classes was fine, but to have the time and luxury to pursue her own work… and maybe by doing so she could finally exorcise Lincoln from her soul by immersing herself totally in her work. And so she agreed.

"And then the fire," she concluded, stealing a glance at Lincoln. "Everything is gone and I'm stuck with a commitment that I can't possibly fulfill. I'd hoped that by getting away I would become magically inspired again." She chuckled derisively.

"Have you tried to paint at all since the fire?"

She shook her head. "Every time I even think about it, all I can see is flames and smell the acrid scent of smoke and the very tools I use to create are the cause of me losing everything. Ironic, isn't it?"

"Was the fire investigated?"

She shrugged. "They said it was a spark of some sort that ignited the paintings downstairs in the gallery, and with all the combustibles in the building, there wasn't much of a chance."

"Hmm. I've never known you to be careless, Desiree. Did you ever think that perhaps the fire was set intentionally?"

Her heart lurched and she snapped her head in his direction.

"No, of course not. Why would anyone do that?"

"People do all kinds of things for reasons that escape

the average person." He waved off the idea. "Just a thought," he murmured, but the notion had taken hold in his mind.

"Desi, remember years ago when we first met and I asked you why you paint? Do you remember what you said?"

"Yes."

"That's what you need—passion, desire, the images to become resurrected and take on life in your mind."

"I know that but—"

"And I'm going to help you get it back."

"Lincoln—"

"There's no getting out of it." He turned to look at her. "Starting tomorrow—at sunrise."

"Sunrise!" She laughed. "You're kidding, right?"

"You can't beat it for inspiration. But in the meantime, let's make a truce."

"Okay. What is it?"

"Starting from today, right now, we forget about the past, forget about us being an us, and start fresh as friends. No strings, no commitments." He pulled the truck to the side of the road and stopped. "Deal?" He held his breath.

She hesitated a moment, wondering how she and Lincoln could ever be "just friends." But at the same time she realized how much she wanted him in her life any way she could have him.

"Deal," she finally agreed.

He stuck out his hand. "My name is Lincoln Davenport, and I own this place."

She placed her hand in his. "Desiree Armstrong… and I'm happy to be here." And she realized as she said the words that she really meant it.

They spent hours walking the beaches, running in and out of the surf, laughing and talking about everything and nothing special, but at the same time they were getting to know each other again as new, changed people.

He told her about some of the eccentric guests who'd come to The Port, and she told him that those same characters had visited her shop. They talked about world affairs, their real opinions about terrorists' threats and the struggling economy and how it affected both of them.

He asked about her family and the renowned family gathering and she told him about her baby sister, Denise, who just moved into yet another new home.

"Another one?" Lincoln laughed. "This makes house number three?"

"Yep. My baby sister changes houses like people lease cars. She gets tired of it, she sells it for a new one. I don't know how her husband deals with it." She shook her head.

"I need her as a client," he said. "I have some land I can sell her."

They laughed.

"You've done marvelous things with this place, Linc. It's idyllic."

"Thanks. I worked really hard to get it the way we… I mean…"

She lowered her head. "I know. I remember," she said softly, looking up at him.

"I didn't mean to bring up the past," he said.

"It's okay. As much as we may want to, we can't entirely avoid the past. It's part of who we are…were."

"You've changed," he said as the understanding settled within him.

"Is that a good thing or a bad thing?"

"We'll have to see, won't we?" He took her hand. "Come on, let's get you back to your place or you won't be about to wake up in…" He checked his watch. "Three hours."

Desiree groaned at the prospect as they walked back hand in hand to the truck. She stole a glance at him from the corner of her eye and her stomach did that little flip thing and she thought how good her hand felt in his.

Chapter 13

If Desiree didn't know better she would swear that a new day came early for the first time in history. But although her body and her eyes felt as if they were filled with lead, her spirit was light and her heart beat with anticipation.

She glanced out of the window at the pale light that peeked through the puffs of clouds. Stretching her long limbs, she pulled herself out of bed and stumbled toward the bathroom.

If Lincoln was remotely like the man she remembered, he would be exactly on time and he would always get that tight look between his eyes when she wasn't ready.

She smiled as she turned on the shower. If she also

remembered correctly she was always able to ease him into compliance with a few well-placed kisses behind his ears and along the cord of his neck. Preferably on the right side.

Desiree stepped under the spray of hot water. Yes, it worked every time. Truth be told, most times she was late on purpose just so that she could keep her skills in top form.

Lathering her skin with honey and almond body wash, she quickly finished up, then rinsed her locks before getting out.

Taking her time, she smoothed body lotion on her arms, legs, hips and thighs and a little extra on her feet and ankles. If there was one thing she couldn't stand, it was ashy feet.

Briefly she stood in front of the closet. Decisions, decisions. Finally she selected an ankle-length gauzy skirt in a pale peach with lemon-yellow splashes, and a yellow handkerchief top that tied behind her neck and around her waist and offered just enough to tantalize the eye without being too suggestive. She added silver teardrop earrings, a hint of lip gloss, peach espadrilles, and she was ready. She squeezed a quarter-sized amount of hair oil in her palms and ran her hands through her damp locks to give them a nice shine.

No sooner had she stood in front of the mirror to take a last look than the knocking on the front door nearly made her jump a foot into the air.

She looked at the door, then herself in the mirror.

What was she thinking? She didn't look like a woman going out to see the sunrise. She looked like a woman attempting to attract a handsome man or at the very least jockey for a hot date.

The knocking came again.

Momentary panic and indecision kept her rooted in place. Maybe she could pretend she wasn't there. If she didn't answer, he'd eventually go away—mad but away. Or maybe she could take everything off, put on her robe and pretend to be sick.

"Desiree! I know you're in there," Lincoln shouted from outside.

She squeezed her eyes shut and stomped her foot in frustration. What was she going to do?

"Breakfast is getting cold and you're going to miss the sunrise," he singsonged.

Desiree blew out a breath. This was silly. There was nothing between her and Lincoln. They were just two old friends sharing the beauty of a sunrise. No commitments. No strings. What did it matter what she had on or what he thought about it?

With that very weak rationale, she pulled herself together and went to the door.

"Sorry to keep you waiting," she said the instant she opened the door. "I was in the bathroom."

Was he staring? He couldn't be sure. But if he was, he didn't care. She was food for the eyes and he was a starving man.

"It was worth it," he murmured, his voice deeper than normal as his gaze strolled over her body.

Heat splashed over her and every nerve ending stood at attention. She remembered that look all too well. It was how he looked at her just before…

"I…uh, I'll wait in the truck," he said, suddenly nervous and uncertain if he would be able to keep from stripping her naked and taking her right there and then if he didn't get away quickly.

Desiree blinked rapidly and held on to the door handle for support. Her thighs trembled and her nipples had hardened to sensitive peaks, blatantly announcing her instant arousal.

How in the world was she supposed to get through spending hours with this man when her body went on high alert just at a glance from him?

She shook her head to clear it, turned and picked up her straw bag from the bed. Well, if there was ever a time to run, it would be right about now, she mused. But the truth was she really didn't want to.

Desiree joined Lincoln at the truck and he nearly tripped over himself getting her door open and helping her inside. She thought it was cute.

"So, did you get any rest?"

"Not enough." She laughed lightly.

"Sorry for keeping you up so late," he said as he made the turn and headed for the beach.

"Oh, I'm not complaining. I…enjoyed it."

Lincoln stole a look at her. "So did I." He paused

and changed the direction of the conversation. "If you roll down your window you can hear the birds getting ready for the day."

Desiree pressed the button at her side and the window glided down. The smell of the ocean immediately filled the car, followed by what sounded like music.

She turned to him and grinned. "Wow. Nothing like mornings on the beach. It's beautiful."

"But not as beautiful as you," he said softly.

Desiree lowered her gaze. "Thank you."

Lincoln reached for the radio and turned it on before he said something else that was out of line.

"Are all the cabins full?" she asked, needing to hear his voice and not that of the radio announcer.

"Yes, our last guest arrived yesterday afternoon. Business has been pretty steady. It's a busy time of the year." He pulled to a stop. "Look." He pointed toward the horizon. "That's what I'm talking about."

The sun poked its head above the horizon, tossing incredible rays of dazzling color across the water. Behind it the sky was still inky in color but began to lighten by degrees as the ball of light slowly ascended and filled the sky. It was pure magic. And watching, one felt insignificant up against the awesome power of the Almighty.

Desiree pressed her hand to her chest, overcome by the splendor before her. This vision was a testament, a

clear indicator that each day was a blessing, a new beginning, a chance to start over.

"Thank you, Lincoln," she whispered.

Chapter 14

They walked slowly along the beach, barefoot, carrying their shoes in their hands and talking softly as the world gently came to life around them.

"When you're not here, where are you?" Desiree asked.

"Oh, I travel, check out new real estate opportunities. I haven't really settled in one place in a long time. I do have an apartment in Manhattan."

She turned to him. "You do? I…we've never run into each other."

"I know. Even though Manhattan is only an island it's a pretty big place, easy to get lost in."

She glanced down at her feet, watching the sand sift

between her toes as they walked. "Did you know where I was?"

"No. I stopped looking, as much as I didn't want to." He pulled in a breath and glanced at her. "I thought it was best. Was it?"

She was thoughtful for a moment. "It's what I said I wanted."

"Was it really, Desiree? Did you really want to erase me out of your life as if I never existed, as if we never existed?"

"I couldn't handle seeing you, Linc. I just couldn't. I had to find a way to move on, to build a new life."

There was so much he wanted to say to her. He wanted to tell her how desperately lonely he'd been, how unhappy. He wanted to tell her that together they could have accomplished so much, that the love they had for each other could have overcome anything. But he wouldn't. At least not now. They'd been together less than an hour and already they were talking about their pasts, breaking the promise they'd made to each other.

"Hungry?" he asked, switching subjects.

She laughed, relieved that the conversation had taken a turn. "Starved."

"I have everything to fix that. Come on." He took her hand and led her back to the truck.

He opened the back door and pulled out a blanket. "Here, take this." He handed the blanket to Desiree, then reached inside and pulled out an electric-blue thermal bag. "Just what the doctor ordered. There's a great spot over there." He pointed toward a cluster of trees just above the beach. "I hate getting sand in my food," he said by way of explaining why they wouldn't be eating on the beach.

"Fine with me."

She followed him up the slight incline until they reached the spot he'd pointed out. Desiree spread the blanket on the grass and Lincoln began unloading the items in the bag: warm, homemade biscuits, fresh fruit, piping-hot coffee, a carafe of freshly squeezed orange juice, tins of jams and jellies, linen napkins, fancy paper plates that looked like the real thing and actual forks and knives, not the plastic ones.

"Wow. I'm impressed." She sat on her haunches and looked over the fare. "Did you toil all night putting this together?" she teased.

"Actually…no." He laughed. "I left a note for our chef when I came in last night to put something together for me. I take it that you like everything."

"Mmm-hmm," she mumbled over a mouthful of biscuit, slathered in apple butter. She reached for a napkin and wiped her mouth. "Do all of your guests get treated so well?"

"We try to make everyone who comes here feel special." He gave her a long look. "Some more special than others." He glanced away and reached for the juice. "I'm sorry, I shouldn't have said that."

"It's okay. Really."

They were silent for a while as they ate, simply relaxing and taking in the sights. There were other early birds who had taken to the ocean for a swim, while others roamed the length of the beach below.

"Do you have plans for the rest of the day?" Lincoln asked.

"Hmm. Not really. I thought maybe I would go into town and check out some of the shops."

"I could show you around…if you wanted me to."

She smiled. "Yeah, I'd like that."

"Then it's a date, or rather a deal. I can pick you up around one if that works for you, just in case you want to rest for a while."

"Perfect." She yawned, then stretched out on the blanket with her face toward the sun, absorbing the warm rays.

Lincoln looked down at her and was again captivated by her innocent beauty. She wasn't what one would consider cover-model pretty. But to him she was the most beautiful woman in the world. A simple smile from her would lighten his day, the sound of her voice would linger in his mind for hours. She was intelligent and fun, sexy and talented. Everything a man could want in a woman. But there was also Desiree's other side, the one who withdrew, shut him out, who would rather face her challenges alone than with a partner. It was that part of her that he'd tried unsuccessfully to penetrate. Yes, they'd both changed in the years that they were apart. Had that part of her changed, as well? He could only hope.

Desiree closed her eyes, enjoying the moment, taking in the atmosphere and the sounds around her. It was all so perfect, she thought. It was a morning that they'd talked of and dreamed about often while they were together. Lincoln had always been so thoughtful and considerate of her needs. He seemed to sense what she wanted even before she did. And yet there was still a part of her that she'd never completely turned over to him. She'd always been afraid to totally let go and give in to the powerful emotions that she'd felt for Lincoln. It was almost as if she were trying to protect herself from getting hurt, even though deep in her heart she believed that he would never hurt her. Ironically, it was the barrier she'd set up that helped her get through her loss and gave her the strength to walk away from him.

But now, being in his presence again, she realized how wrong she had been and how much time had been wasted. Yet, she was still uncertain if she could cross that final line and let him totally into her heart and mind, into that corner of herself that felt less than whole. He saw her as perfect, totally wonderful and capable. In truth she wasn't and if she let him into her life and her heart once again, how would he react when he knew the truth. She didn't want to risk that. So, she would make the most of the time they had together, and when it was over she would go back to her life and he would go back to his.

That's simply the way it had to be.

Chapter 15

Carl slowly hung up the phone. The fire marshal wanted to investigate the fire further before making a final determination. That was troubling.

He had a meeting with the accountants in two hours. The insurance adjusters needed his signature and his investors wanted to know what he planned to do about their money. Everything would fall apart if anything out of order was discovered. He didn't want to contemplate what he would do then.

He ran his hand across his clean-shaven jaw. And he still had no idea where Desiree was. He pushed back from his desk and stood. There was one person who would know. He should have gone there first.

* * *

The knock on Rachel's door caused her to look up from examining some stones laid out on a black velvet cloth on her desk.

"Come in." She held a finely cut opal up to the light.

"Hi, Rae, sorry to disturb you. There's a Carl Hampton here to see you. I told him you were busy, but he says it's urgent."

Slowly Rachel put the stone down. "Everything is urgent with Carl," she grumbled. "Tell him I'll be with him in a minute."

"Sure," Felicia said and closed the door behind her.

Rachel collected the stones and returned them to the case, then put it in her desk drawer and locked it. The last person she wanted to see or talk to was Carl Hampton. He could only want one thing. She was sure it wasn't a pure social call. There was something about Carl that rubbed her the wrong way. She couldn't tell Desiree often enough what a mistake it was to have gotten involved with him in the first place.

She put on her jacket that she'd hung on the back of her chair and went out front.

As always, Carl was impeccably dressed in an obviously expensive steel-gray suit, a pale gray shirt, and a burgundy-and-gray striped tie. His thin mustache was trimmed to perfection, outlining his equally thin upper lip with his blue eyes as cold as a February morning.

"Carl. This is a surprise."

"Is it?" He walked toward her. "I would think you'd be expecting me."

"Why in the world would I be expecting you?"

"Enough with the pleasantries. I need to talk to you."

"Funny, I thought that's what we were doing." Rachel folded her arms.

Carl cut a look in Felicia's direction. "Alone."

Rachel pursed her lips. "Fine. We can talk in my office." She led him to the back but didn't offer him a seat. He took one anyway. "What is this about, Carl?"

"It's about Desiree. I need to talk to her."

"I'm pretty sure if Desiree wanted to talk to you she would have contacted you by now."

His face flushed crimson. "I don't think you or Desiree understand the seriousness of what's going on here," he said, struggling to control his spiraling temper. "I am up to my eyeballs in debt and paperwork. I have investors that want answers."

"You're a seasoned businessman, Carl. I'm pretty sure that you're insured up to your eyeballs, as well." She braced her hand on her hip.

He clenched his jaw and raised his chin. "The fire marshal called me today."

"And?"

"They want to investigate the fire further before signing off. There seems to be some idea that it may have been arson."

Rachel's heart thumped in her chest. "Arson? That's ridiculous."

"They don't seem to think so. If it's discovered that it was arson, I can forget the insurance money that I'll need to pay off the investors until we find out who did it, if ever. Not to mention what I'll lose on the property."

"I still don't see what this has to do with Desiree," Rachel said, hoping she'd disguised the worry in her voice.

"I need to talk to her. I need to find out if she heard anything, saw anything or anyone suspicious. And I need to find out if she's going to be able to paint—to put enough pieces together for a show. At least I'd be able to appease the investors if I could guarantee that much before they call in their notes."

In the time that Rachel knew Carl, she'd never seen him ruffled. If he was this upset and it wasn't a ploy to get to Desiree, then maybe she should consider taking it seriously.

"I'll tell you what I'll do. I'll get a message to Desiree and hopefully she'll contact you. Fair enough?"

"Thank you. Please try to impress upon her how important this is."

"I'll do my best but I won't guarantee anything."

Carl nodded and walked out.

Rachel sat at her desk going over what Carl said. What if it was arson? But the real questions were who and why?

Reluctantly, Rachel picked up the phone and dialed The Port.

"Good afternoon, I'm trying to reach one of your guests, Desiree Armstrong."

"Just a moment, I'll ring her room."

Rachel listened to the phone ring on the other end until the automated voice mail service kicked in. She left a message.

"Hey, Des. It's me, Rae. Just checking on you, girl. Hope you're having fun. Give a sistah a call when you get a minute." She hung up wondering if she should have been more insistent about having Desiree call her back. But at the same time she didn't want to worry her. She sighed deeply. Desi would call, and when she did they would talk, really talk.

"Where to first?" Desiree asked, as Lincoln helped her into the Navigator.

"I thought I would show you some of the boutique shops. I know how much you like vintage clothing. There are a couple of really nice galleries." He stole a glance at her. She didn't react. "And then I thought we could take a tour of the museum."

"I've heard about it. It's a landmark, isn't it?"

"Yes, it has a lot of historical significance to the African-American community."

"I'm looking forward to it."

"Then dinner if you like," he said, his tone hopeful. "B. Smith's is perfect. You'll love it."

Breakfast, even lunch, was one thing. Dinner inevitably took things to another level, Desiree thought. Was she ready?

"Sounds good. If we're not too worn out by then," she added with caution.

"We'll take the day as it comes." He turned to her. "Remember, no strings, no commitments."

"Right." She wondered how long that would last.

Chapter 16

As he'd promised, Lincoln took her to all the shops, where she was compelled to purchase a denim skirt with fringes, a funky leather motorcycle jacket, a tie-dyed shirt, and a bracelet and choker set of sterling silver.

"You have quite a haul," Lincoln joked, toting her purchases to the truck.

Desiree giggled. "You got me out of there just in time. I had my eye on that raccoon collar."

Lincoln groaned. "Timing is key," he said.

"Where to now?"

"Well, the art gallery is just around that bend."

Her stomach twirled. Art gallery. "Uh…"

He put his hand on her shoulder and looked down

into her eyes. "We don't have to go, Desi, if it makes you uncomfortable. I just thought—"

"No, it's okay," she said, fighting back a wave of nausea.

"Are you sure?"

She nodded. If her goal was to come here to get her act and her head together, this had to be part of the treatment program. "It's fine, really. I need to see what others are doing."

"Okay, then let's go."

When Desiree stepped inside the doors of the Grenning Gallery, she immediately thought she would feel overwhelmed or panicked. But she wasn't. Instead, a sort of calm flowed through her as if she'd finally stepped out of an unfamiliar world into a new one.

She drifted away from Lincoln and began examining the small clay sculptures that sat on round wood tables, the handcrafted jewelry tucked away behind glass cases and the paintings on the wall that varied from traditional water and mountain scenes to the totally abstract.

The gallery wasn't large by any means, but it offered a wide array of selections for tastes on a variety of levels.

Lincoln stood to the side and watched her as she went from one station to another, examining the hangings and checking out the artists' names. He could almost hear her making astute observations about each one. He smiled as he saw her come to life, the animation and light was back in her eyes. He'd been reluctant to bring her, but in his gut he believed this was the best medicine. The only way to beat your fears is to face them. That's what his father always told him before he died, and those were words he lived by.

Desiree turned in Lincoln's direction, a broad smile on her face. She rushed over to him, and before he knew what happened, she'd wrapped him in her arms.

"Thank you," she whispered against his chest. "Thank you so much."

He felt her shudder and he eased her back to look into her eyes. Tears glistened on her lashes. "Are you okay?"

She bobbed her head. "Yes," she uttered on a strangled breath. "A part of me died that night. At least I thought it did. I'd felt so lost and frightened all the time that I wanted to stay as far away as possible from the thing that I loved." She looked up at him. "But I'm finally beginning to realize that I have nothing to fear, Lincoln." Her eyes slowly rolled over his face. "Nothing. Not my art…not you."

His stomach knotted. "Do you really mean that?"

"Yes, I do." She stepped a bit closer. "Kiss me, Lincoln. Right here, right now," she said in an almost urgent whisper.

The corner of his mouth lifted. "With pleasure."

Slowly he lowered his head until his lips touched hers, once, twice, until he captured her mouth. Time shifted as she opened her mouth to receive the exploration of his tongue. A soft moan rose from her center and entered his.

He thought kissing her again would be the same, that the same raw emotions would overwhelm him. But that was not the case. This was new, different, even more powerful than before. It stunned him with its intensity and the rumbling of emotions that shifted from his head to his heart to his loins. He loved her. He knew that. More than ever, and he would do whatever he must in order to have her back in his life—fully.

Desiree's head spun and a warmth like that of being under the summer sun swelled through her. She held on, fearing that the sudden weakness in her knees would soon have her in a heap on the floor. It didn't matter where they were or who saw them, she thought through a haze. All that mattered was the here and now, connecting with Lincoln again. Feeling him, experiencing him again. To hell with the promises they'd made about strings and commitments. She wanted him and she would battle her demons in order to have him.

Giggling from behind them slowly drew them apart. Desiree looked over her shoulder to see a little boy, about six years old, pointing at them to a teenaged girl who looked to be his older sister.

"You have to excuse my little brother," the girl said. "He thinks everything is funny." She tugged him by the arm and they walked away.

Desiree ducked her head and laughed, then looked up at Lincoln. "I guess we did cause a bit of a stir."

"I'm willing to go for round two and see who else we can stir up," Lincoln said with a spark of mischief in his dark brown eyes.

She tapped his arm, then slid hers under it. "Come on. I think we've done enough for today."

They had started out when Desiree stopped short.

"Ms. McKay?" Desiree asked, recognizing the woman from her shop.

For a moment the woman looked flustered. "Do I know you?" She gave Desiree a cautious smile.

"We met a few weeks ago. You came into my shop to pick up a gift for your daughter."

The woman frowned in confusion. "I think you have me mixed up with someone else. Sorry." She walked away.

Desiree followed her with her eyes as the woman exited the gallery and headed for a navy blue Lexus.

"Who was that?" Lincoln asked.

Desiree was silent as she watched the car drive off.

"Desi? Are you okay? Who was that?"

She briskly shook her head and looked at Lincoln. "Sorry. I thought it was someone I'd met at my gallery. But I guess I was wrong," she said slowly.

Lincoln put his arm around her shoulder. "Hey, you know how they say we all look alike."

Desiree chuckled. "Yeah, I guess you're right." She dismissed the episode and turned to Lincoln. "So… where to now?"

He put his arm around her waist. "I don't know about

you, but I'm starved. There's a great little outdoor café about a block away."

"I'm already there."

They walked out of the gallery and headed down the strip talking about their day so far, and Desiree gave Lincoln her blow-by-blow impressions of the paintings she'd seen.

"Tomorrow, if you're up for it, we'll visit the Whale Museum. Sorry we couldn't get to it today…but since you spent so much time shopping…"

She nudged him in the ribs with her elbow. "Watch it, buddy."

"What did I say?" he moaned, pleading innocence.

"I heard that shopping barb. There was a distinct undertone to your voice that bordered on cynical."

"Me! Cynical about you shopping? I'm wounded."

"You will be if you don't watch it," she playfully warned. "Now, feed me!"

He tossed his head back and laughed, truly happy inside and out. He bowed as he opened the restaurant door. "After you, my love."

Desiree's heart stuttered in her chest. She looked at him and their gazes locked for a hot second with the longing evident in both their eyes.

"I said it and I meant it," he said, his voice low and very convincing.

Desiree took a breath, hesitated, then stepped inside. If this was what a day together was like, she thought, her mind racing, what would a long, lazy night bring?

Chapter 17

"You wouldn't be the first building owner to work things out to get the insurance money," Richard Wells, the insurance adjuster, said, making some notes on a pad.

"I'm sure you're joking. So I'll take it as such. If you knew your business as well as you claim, Mr. Wells, you would know that I don't need the insurance money. That's for slum lords."

Mr. Wells looked up from his notes. "You'd be surprised," he said smugly.

Carl chose to ignore him. He had more important things on his mind. He had yet to hear from Desiree. And the fire marshal had called back to say that the investigators would be going back over the debris in the morning. He couldn't hold everyone off forever.

"Until we get the final paperwork from the fire department, I'm afraid we can't pay off on the claim, Mr. Hampton."

"I'm sure that everything is in order. It was an accident."

"We'll wait for the report." He gathered his papers and stuck them in a cheap, fake-leather portfolio. "I'll be in touch." He stood and left the office.

Carl sat for several moments. That did not go well, he thought. And he had yet to meet with his investors. He checked his watch. He had an hour.

Rachel paced the floor of her apartment. She'd left her office several hours earlier in the hope that she would hear from Desiree. Periodically she picked up the phone to check and make sure it was actually working.

Why hadn't she called? The whole notion that someone deliberately set the fire chilled her to the bone. Who could want to hurt Desiree that badly? She could have been killed. Desiree had no enemies that she could think of. Everyone who met her liked her.

Could it be yet another ploy by Carl to bind Desiree to him for real? The idea began to take shape in her head. Carl Hampton was a control freak, and whether Desiree realized it or not, Carl wanted more from her than her paintings.

What man would buy a loft and gallery space and give it to someone simply to get them to paint if he wasn't looking for something in return? No one. But would he go so far as to set fire to the place? Why? To teach Desiree a lesson?

Rachel continued to pace and slowly shook her head. *Why won't she call?*

"Thanks for a wonderful day," Desiree said as they pulled to a stop in front of her cabin.

"I'm glad you decided to join me." He hesitated. "I… uh…have something for you." He walked around to the back of the truck, opened the hood and pulled out an easel, several canvases and a plastic shopping bag of paints and brushes.

"Lincoln…what is all this?" Her eyes widened in disbelief.

"I thought that if you were suddenly inspired…"

Slowly she walked toward him and looked everything over. She ran her hand across the easel and suddenly her heart thumped as recognition took hold.

Her gaze jerked toward him. "This…this is my easel. Where—"

"I never got rid of it," he said quietly. "You left it in the back of the closet in our old apartment. I kept it."

"All these years?" she asked in awe.

He nodded.

Her eyes filled. "But why?"

"It was all I had left of you, Desi. And now that I've found you again, I think it belongs with its rightful owner."

Without thinking, she pressed her body flush against

his and wrapped her arms around him. She struggled to speak over the lump in her throat.

"I don't know what to say," she whispered against his chest.

He stroked her hair, then her back. "Just say that you'll try to paint again. Even if all you do is throw some colors against the canvas."

She laughed, then eased back and looked up at him.

With the pads of his thumbs he brushed away the tears from her cheeks. "Will you?"

She swallowed. "I'll try."

He caressed her cheek. "That's all anyone can do is give it their best shot."

"Can you help me take these inside?"

"My pleasure."

"I think I'll put the easel by the sliding doors. Great light comes in during the early morning."

Lincoln smiled and did as instructed. "What about the paints and the canvases?"

"Hmm." She walked toward the closet and pulled it open. "The paints can go on the floor." She turned and scanned the room, then pointed to the wall next to the dresser. "The canvases can go over there."

She put her hands on her hips and stood in the center of the room while Lincoln placed the canvases against the wall.

"Anything else, Sarge?" he asked, giving her a mock salute.

She pursed her lips. "Very funny."

"This is the Desiree that I remember," he said, leaning casually against the wall unit. "Excited, smiling, giving off that energy like no one else can."

"I have you to thank for that."

He shook his head in denial. "I only offered you the tools. The rest is up to you."

She took a seat on the side of the bed. "I know." She sighed deeply. "Why did you really keep the easel, Linc?"

He slung his hands in his pockets and looked directly into her questioning eyes. "After you left, I was a mess. I didn't eat, didn't sleep, I drank too much. All I wanted to do was find a way to make things right between us again. But I couldn't. You wouldn't let me."

"Lincoln—"

"Finally I decided that I couldn't live in the same place we shared any longer. And maybe in a new place, with a fresh start, I could forget all about you." He clenched his jaw as the old wounds painfully reopened. "I was packing up a couple of days before the movers were set to come and I was pulling stuff out of that hall closet where we tossed all the things we couldn't figure out what to do with."

They laughed absently at the memory.

"And there in the back of the closet was the easel. The first one you ever bought. When I saw it sitting there, everything came rushing back. All those mornings when I would wake up and you were sitting in that raggedy sweatshirt with the paint stains in front of the window with the most intense expression on your face while you painted. And when you would hear me stir you'd turn toward me and the smile and the light that sparkled in your eyes would fill me up."

For a moment he looked away and then back at her.

"I took the easel out of the closet and suddenly you were back with me again. At least a part of you." He gave a short laugh. "I know I must sound like a fool telling you all this, hanging on to an inanimate object like some kind of trophy, but it gave me what I needed to move on with my life. When I would see you sitting there in the morning, it was a symbol of possibility. And having that part of you allowed me to feel that again. That's why I kept it, and that's why I want you to have it."

Desiree covered her face with her hands and wept.

"Desi." Lincoln sat beside her and gathered her in his arms. "Don't cry, babe. I didn't tell you all that to upset you."

"I've been so damned selfish and self-centered," she uttered between her sobs. "I wouldn't allow myself to think about how what I'd done made you feel, what it was doing to you. It was easier to run."

"It's okay," he whispered. "It's the past. I shouldn't have brought it up."

"No," she said, her voice cracking. "I need to hear it. I need to understand it." She sniffed and wiped at her eyes. "It was so unfair to you." She looked at him through tear-filled eyes. "How can I ever make it right?"

"You can start by changing clothes and getting ready for our dinner date at B. Smith's." He smiled gently at her and her heart seemed to shift in her chest.

She nodded her head and grinned, then wiped away the last of her tears. "All this for a dinner date?" She sniffed. "Will you stop at nothing?"

He shrugged and gave her a boyish grin. "Can't blame a man for tryin'. But you know what, Ms. Armstrong?" He pulled her to her feet. "You ain't seen nothing yet."

Chapter 18

Alone in her bedroom, Desiree trembled as she stared at the easel by the window. She wrapped her arms around her body to stave off the shudders that ran amok up and down her body. Lincoln's words echoed in her head. To him the easel was a symbol of possibility.

At one time in her life it meant the same thing to her. But now it symbolized loss and fear. She couldn't tell him that. Not after all he'd said and all he'd been through.

She was deeply touched by the gesture, understanding that Lincoln was only doing what he thought was best. The truth was she'd done everything in her power not to scream. Her tears were not tears of joy but of terror. Terror that the nightmares would now return with a vengeance, since the symbols of her near destruction were within eyesight.

Slowly Desiree sat down at the foot of the bed and covered her face with her hands. Her heart raced.

Rationally, she understood that in order to beat your fears you must confront them. Lincoln was one. She'd allowed the door to her heart to crack open, letting in the light of his smile, the comfort of his warmth into her soul, the memories into her mind. But she wasn't ready to let him in all the way and wasn't sure when she would be—if ever.

She experienced a momentary bout of bravery by allowing herself to admit out loud that she still loved him, still wanted him. To take it further than that—a thought, an utterance in the confines of her room? She wasn't ready, and she never should have led him on by kissing him.

She'd been trying to prepare herself for the next step with him when she felt stronger inside, more certain of her emotions. She knew that if she rekindled a relationship with Lincoln she would have to tell him the whole truth, tell him everything. She hadn't reached that point yet.

Desiree stole a glance at the easel. Now this. Whatever bravado she felt had been pulled out from under her like a rug. Lincoln would undoubtedly expect her to start painting—or tossing paint at the bare minimum. The thought of picking up a brush made her head spin.

The scent of turpentine and paint suddenly filled

her nostrils, followed by the acrid odor of smoke and burning wood. She ran to the bathroom and leaned over the bowl. Her stomach knotted, rose and fell as a cold, clammy sweat claimed her body. She stayed on her hands and knees for what felt like an eternity as wave upon wave of that night rushed up from her belly and released itself.

On shaky legs she finally rose from the cool black-and-white-tiled floor and turned on the cold water in the sink, splashing it on her face. She dampened a cloth and pressed it to the back of her neck until she began to feel human.

Desiree looked at herself in the mirror. Rings of black underlined her eyes, giving her a cartoonish look. Her face was flushed and her eyes glassy.

The doctors called what just happened to her an olfactory hallucination. She called it crazy. It was making her crazy.

She hadn't experienced an episode since before her arrival at The Port. They'd been nightly visitors prior, unwanted guests that tramped through her mind at will.

This was one of the worst.

She took one of the washcloths and scrubbed her face clean of makeup, brushed her teeth and rinsed her mouth. If she intended to keep her dinner date with Lincoln she'd have to pull herself together. She braced her hands on the sides of the sink and took long, deep breaths, but she didn't have the will or the strength to do much more than that.

Desiree returned to the bedroom and picked up the phone, noticing for the first time the flashing red light indicating that she had a message waiting. The only person who knew she was there was Rachel. Maybe she'd call her later. Rachel knew her much too well and would immediately sense that something was wrong, and she wasn't up for dancing around what would surely be Rachel's relentless line of questioning.

Instead she called the main house and left a message for Lincoln. She was more tired than she realized, she'd said, and hoped that he would understand her canceling their dinner.

With that done, she got out of her clothes, put on a gown and crawled beneath the cool covers, silently praying that her guests would leave her be for a few hours.

"Oh, there you are, Mr. D.," Terri said as Lincoln walked into the reception area, whistling. "I have a message for you." She handed him a slip of paper. "I'm heading home. Grace is here and I brought her up to date on everything." She slung her purse over her left shoulder and angled her head to the side. His whistling stopped. "Are you okay, Mr. D.?"

Lincoln read the words again, before finally looking up at Terri. He crushed the paper into a ball and tossed it into the wicker wastebasket near the desk.

"I'm fine. Have a good evening," he muttered absently and walked off to his office.

Sitting behind his desk, Lincoln recapped the entire

day with Desiree. Everything seemed fine. She was happy, smiling, and she acted as if she still cared. The kiss…was that just, what, an act? A means of testing the waters?

She'd changed her mind for a reason. He'd left her barely an hour ago. What happened?

Get a grip, man, he admonished himself. Maybe she really was tired. He shouldn't take it personally. He pushed away from the desk, stood and walked to the window. With more force than needed he pushed the curtains aside. Damn it, he did take it personally.

"What are you trying to pull, Desiree? What's really going on with you?"

Chapter 19

Cynthia crossed, then uncrossed her legs before positioning herself in the stiff wooden chair.

Mr. Wells, the insurance adjuster, took off his glasses and set them next to his yellow legal pad on his desk.

"Ms. Hastings, I want to go over some information with you about the fire."

"I've already told the fire department everything I know." She tugged at the hem of her jacket, pulling it taut against her slender frame.

Mr. Wells smiled. "I know. But for the purposes of my investigation I need to ask my own questions. So please bear with me."

Cynthia sucked on her bottom lip with her teeth

and lifted her chin. "Fine, but you're just wasting your time."

"Why don't you let me be the judge of that? Now, tell me, did you notice anything odd about Ms. Armstrong lately?"

Cynthia frowned, taken aback by the question. She leaned slightly forward. "Desiree? What do you mean 'odd'?"

Mr. Wells linked his short fingers together. "Was she overly anxious?" He shrugged slightly. "Nervous or forgetful lately?"

"I…" She paused for a moment. "Well…she had been on edge recently," she offered, hesitating over each word.

"What do you mean?"

"She was behind in her work. Mr. Hampton was calling and dropping by every day, and it was really bugging her. She was trying to get her work together for her very first exhibit and she didn't think she would have it done in time."

"I see." He leaned back in his chair. "Did she confide in you about how she was feeling—this pressure she was under by Mr. Hampton, for instance?"

"She'd mentioned something once or twice. She didn't come right out and say anything, but I knew," she added.

"How is that?"

"Desiree is always pleasant, easy to work with. But the closer she got to the exhibit date, and the more Mr.

Hampton kept dropping by, the more short-tempered she became. She started forgetting things and blaming me for orders that were missing or incorrect when she was the one who'd made the mistakes."

"Interesting," he murmured and made some notes on his pad. "Tell me, Ms. Hastings, if she were unable to complete the work in time, what would have happened?"

"The show would have to be canceled, of course, and Mr. Hampton would lose thousands of dollars. He'd made a major investment."

"Do you think Ms. Armstrong was capable of setting the fire herself to get out of the commitment she couldn't keep—get herself off the hook so to speak?"

Cynthia pulled in a breath. "I don't know," she said, inching out every word. "I suppose anything is possible. Just hard to believe that Desiree would do something like that."

Mr. Wells slid his glasses back onto the bridge of his nose and glanced at her over the top of them. "And where were you on the night of the fire?"

Her nostrils suddenly flared as if she couldn't quite breathe. "I was at home," she stated, her tone sharp and precise. She clenched her hands together on her lap.

Mr. Wells made a note on his pad. "Did Ms. Armstrong and Mr. Hampton get along well?"

"Yes."

"Were they more than…business associates?"

Cynthia stiffened her shoulders. "I really wouldn't know."

"You're a very intelligent woman. You may not know for certain, but I'm sure you can guess."

"Do I know if they were more than just business associates? No. But as I said earlier, anything is possible."

Abruptly, he stood and extended his hand, effectively ending their conversation. "You've been very helpful, Ms. Hastings."

Caught off guard by the swift change in direction, Cynthia needed a moment to react. Finally she shook his hand as she stood up.

"If I have any further questions, I'll be sure to be in touch."

She nodded and reached for her purse, then turned to leave.

"Oh, and, Ms. Hastings," he called out just as her hand cupped the doorknob.

She glanced at him from over her shoulder.

"If you think of anything, I do expect that you'd give me a call."

She looked at him a second, then opened the door and walked out.

Cynthia stepped into the elevator. Realizing that she was alone, she leaned back against the wall and shut her eyes. Was it possible that Desiree was responsible?

"What's the holdup with the insurance payout?" Sylvester Ward, one of Carl's major investors, asked.

Over the years, Carl had made a practice of finding

people with money and convincing them that investing in his various enterprises would always be worth their while. Sylvester was one of his earliest and most long-standing "partners." He'd pumped millions of dollars into numerous ventures over the years This was small potatoes to Sly, but for some unknown reason he had a real bug up his behind about his money. And he was making Carl's life hell.

Carl's accountant spoke up.

"We're working out the details, Mr. Ward. In cases like this, the insurance company wants to cross every *t*—"

"I don't want to hear that crap. I want to know how and when I'm going to get my money back." He pulled out a cigar from the inside breast pocket of his jacket and snipped off the end with a deadly looking little gadget, then lit up and blew a puff of noxious smoke into the air.

Carl hated the smell of cigars, especially the cheap ones that Sylvester smoked. One would think that with all the money he made he would invest in a good cigar, one that didn't have the stench of death.

The accountant coughed once and quickly apologized.

Sylvester pointed the cigar at Carl. "We've been working together for a lot of years, Carl. Made a lot of money together. But I'm going to be honest with you. I don't like how this is shaping up. I don't like that the insurance company is dragging its feet, and from what

I hear the fire department is questioning whether or not it was arson. I can't have my name attached to any scandals, Carl. I'm sure you understand."

The air in the conference room evaporated. A cloud of smoke hung over the table like fog over L.A. during rush hour in the summer.

Carl blinked rapidly to ease the sting in his eyes.

"Sylvester, I understand. And I'm sure you understand that my hands are tied. I'm sure this will all be worked out in no time."

"That's not good enough. You see, I have other investments. I need my money."

"Be reasonable. If everything had gone according to schedule, you wouldn't have gotten a return on your money for at least another six months."

Sylvester blew more smoke into the air. "Since the situation has changed, the deal has changed. I want out and I want my money." He stood.

His six-foot-six, three-hundred-pound body cast a long shadow across the table. "Tell you what. Since we've been friends for so long, I'll give you a week from today. I'll expect to see you in my office, say around six. We could go out for drinks afterward." He smiled and his gold right incisor gleamed through the cloud. "Deal?"

Carl stood. It took all he had to remain calm and civil. "Deal." He shrugged slightly. "That's fair. It will be all cleared up by then anyway." He came around the table to walk Sylvester to the door. He patted him heartily on the back. "Always a pleasure, Sly."

Sylvester chuckled. "Let it stay that way." He opened the door and walked out in a cloud of smoke.

Chapter 20

Desiree woke up the following morning achy and foggy. All night she had recurring dreams of running. She ran through the woods, across the white sands of the beach, through the streets of New York, away from everything and everyone that was familiar. Her mother, aunts and sisters chased her. Rachel was in pursuit. She could hear the pounding of Lincoln's footsteps behind her. But she was too fast for them, too clever. She outsmarted them all. She hid behind a facade of independence, self-reliance and resiliency. They couldn't penetrate that, couldn't get beyond her protective shield.

By the end of the dream, moments before the sun crested the horizon, Desiree found herself standing alone, with nowhere to go.

She lay in bed staring up at the ceiling as slivers of light crept across the floor through the thin slats of the blinds. How could she continue to live this way in a constant state of fear and denial? She'd hoped that getting away would somehow lift the weight that sat so heavily on her soul. All it had done was force her to realize that she was tired of running but she was still too afraid to stop. If she did all that everyone believed of her, and what she'd convinced herself of, everything would come crashing down around her and then she truly would have nothing.

Lincoln awoke with the sun, barely having slept a full two hours during the night. More than once he'd thought of going to Desiree's cabin and confronting her once and for all.

She was hiding something. He was sure of that. But what? He understood her trauma about the fire. But he could not understand what was happening between them. He wanted to help her in any way that he could, but the instant he got close she pushed him away. It had always been that way between them, long before they lost the baby. But afterward she'd gotten worse, more withdrawn and closed, until he couldn't reach her at all.

What else had happened in her life that made her so fearful of living it to the fullest, to embrace it with the same fierce passion that she'd once had for her work? He knew in his gut that something in her past was at the root of it. But what?

Pulling himself up from the bed, he went into the bathroom, took a quick shower and got dressed. He was going to get some answers one way or the other.

He went to his dresser, pulled out some necessary items and tossed them into an overnight bag. He grabbed his jacket, wallet and car keys and headed out.

Grace was still on duty when he walked into the main house.

"Well, you're up early," Grace said, looking up from the newspaper. She took a sip from her coffee mug. "Anything I can do for you?"

"I'm going out of town. It may be a few days."

"Oh." Her brows rose in question but she didn't pose one, unlike Terri, who would have unleashed a line of questions.

"I hope to be back early next week. Let Terri and the rest of the staff know. Josh will have to do the drop-offs and pickups of the guests while I'm gone."

"I'll tell him."

"You have my cell phone number in case you really need me."

"I'm sure everything will be fine," Grace said in her usual casual manner.

"Thanks, Grace."

"Drive safely, Mr. Davenport."

"I will."

He walked out and hurried off to his truck. Barring anything major on the roads he should be in North Carolina in eight hours. And he had no intention of coming back until he had some answers.

Desiree stood in the open doorway of her cabin and noticed Lincoln's black Navigator drive off toward the main road.

Inexplicably she had a sudden sense of foreboding as if something that would drastically change the course of her life was about to happen.

She started to run, barefoot, toward the road. She could still see Lincoln's truck. But he was putting more and more distance between them.

She ran faster, calling his name in a frantic plea. But he never stopped, never looked back, and then he made the turn onto the main road and was gone.

Desiree finally slowed and came to a stop. She leaned against a tree, breathing hard. She was being ridiculous, she silently scolded herself. He was probably driving into town for supplies or something.

She bent over and braced her hands on her knees, pulling in deep breaths of salt-tinged air. Straightening up, she looked around. There was not another soul to be seen. And just as in her dream, she was totally alone.

Rachel listened to the phone ring until the voice mail service came on. She tapped her foot and checked her watch. Where in the hell could Desiree be at this time of the morning?

"Your car is outside to take you to the airport, Rae!" Felicia called out.

"Tell him I'll be right there."

"Desi, it's me, Rae. I've been trying to reach you. Please give me a call on my cell phone. I'm on my way to the airport. Have a business deal in London. My flight is at nine. Try to call before then. If not I will try to reach you when I get to the Carly Hotel. Bye."

She grabbed her purse and headed out. Maybe something worked out between her and Lincoln after all, she thought with a smile as she settled into the limo. What other explanation could there be for Desiree not to be in her own bed at six-thirty in the morning?

Chapter 21

It was nearly three o'clock by the time Lincoln spotted the exit for Charlotte, North Carolina. From that point he was traveling on pure instinct and vague memories of having visited Desiree's family years earlier.

He probably should have called first, he thought, coming to a stop at a red light. But if southern hospitality was as it had always been, then drop-in guests were still welcome. The light turned green and he drove through the intersection looking for any landmarks that would give him his bearings.

Lincoln wound his way in and out of downtown Charlotte until he reached the outskirts of town. This was where it got kind of tricky, he thought, remembering a time when he rode around in circles for an hour before he finally gave up and asked for directions.

What in the world would he say when he got there? he suddenly wondered as he turned onto Queens Drive, the reality of his impulsive act finally sinking in. Desiree's mother would think that something was wrong—if she even remembered who he was. But what if she'd moved or was out of town? He had no idea how to reach any of Desiree's sisters.

But he reasoned, if it came to that, someone in Charlotte would know where to find them. The Armstrong family was a little kingdom and everyone knew everyone else.

Nothing like New York, he mused as the lush green scenery sped past his windows. You could live right next door to someone for years and never know them by name. It must be nice to have the kind of sense of community that people shared outside of major urban cities. He always wondered why Desiree had been so hell-bent on not returning, and taking up residence in a city that bred anonymity. There was a reason, and the answers were here.

Not wanting to take a chance on spending the rest of the day driving in circles, he pulled into a gas station to get directions. He hopped out of his truck and walked over to where an attendant was washing the windows of another customer's van.

"Be right with ya," the man said as he meticulously wiped away all traces of water from the windshield.

"No rush. I just have a question."

In towns like this the gas station attendants were equivalent to the bartenders in New York. They knew everyone and everything, Lincoln thought.

The attendant hooked the rag onto a loop on his pants, tapped the hood of the van as the driver pulled off. He turned to Lincoln and pulled his cap down low over his eyes to hide from the sun.

"Now what can I do for you? Need directions? I can tell you're not from around here."

Lincoln chuckled. "That obvious?"

"Folks stop here for three reasons, gas, gossip and directions. You gave me the idea you didn't need gas when you said you needed to ask me something—that could only mean directions. I don't recognize your face, so you couldn't be coming around to catch up on gossip." He shrugged. "Directions. That and the New York plates," he added, pointing to the Navigator. He glanced up at Lincoln through the glare of the sun.

Lincoln shook his head and chuckled. "I was looking for the Armstrong house."

A grin broke across the man's face as if he'd been told he just won the lottery.

"Well, why didn't you just say so?" He squinted as if to get Lincoln into focus and pointed a grease-stained finger at him. "You a relative?"

"No. Not exactly. Friend of the family."

The man took off his cap and scratched his head. "Seems to me if you were a friend of the family they would have given you directions and you'd know where you were going."

This wasn't going to be easy. Maybe this guy doubled as the local sheriff, too.

"Actually, I haven't been here in a while. I'm…was engaged to Mrs. Armstrong's daughter, Desiree."

The man's brows shot up to his hairline. "Oh, you're the fella," he said as if he held some secret he didn't want to share. He placed his cap back on his head and stroked his stubbled chin. "Hmm. Well, that's all in the past now anyway."

"What's all in the past?"

The old man looked at Lincoln from the corner of his eyes, sizing him up. "They took it pretty hard when she broke the news that she wasn't getting married. Those Armstrong women have a real strong sense of family. If I remember right, it nearly killed her mother when she found out."

He had to be exaggerating, Lincoln thought, but kept quiet.

"Matter of fact, poor Desiree is the only one who ain't hitched." He shot Lincoln a look of accusation. "Nice girl like that should have a husband."

"My feelings exactly," Lincoln quickly offered, sensing that he was venturing on very touchy territory. It was becoming pretty plain that the Armstrongs and possibly everyone else in town somehow believed the breakup was all his fault.

"I was hoping to talk to Mrs. Armstrong, straighten things out."

"Don't you think you waited a mighty long time to straighten things out?"

The old man's skepticism wasn't lost on Lincoln. "Well, a few things have happened since then."

"Oh yeah, like what?" He leaned against a gas pump as if he was ready to settle down for a long story.

"I'd really rather talk to Mrs. Armstrong about it," Lincoln replied, keeping his tone light and friendly.

"Hmm." He looked Lincoln over. "I guess I could tell you where she lives." He eased off the pump and walked toward the station's exit. "Make a left up at the second tree. Take that road down about a mile. You'll see a church on the right-hand side. Go past the church and make two lefts. You'll be right there." He glanced up at Lincoln from beneath the beak of his soiled cap. "Got all that or you need me to write it down?"

Lincoln bit back a chuckle. "I got it. Thanks."

"Anytime. The name's Wally. Stop by on your way out. I'll give you a good deal on some gas and wash that pretty truck down for you."

"Thanks, Wally, I'll keep that in mind."

"What's your name, son?" he asked as Lincoln climbed back into the truck.

"Lincoln Davenport." He turned the key in the ignition and the engine kicked to life.

"Yep, you're the one," he muttered as Lincoln drove off.

* * *

Wally's directions were right on point. In less than ten minutes Lincoln was pulling up to the Armstrong property. He came to a stop at the top of the road that led to the house. It looked very much like what he remembered from the few times he'd visited during the family reunions and once during Christmas.

The white-framed house was a two-story structure with windows that wrapped around the front with the standard porch complete with rocking chair and a few azalea bushes on either side of the steps. It was plain by anyone's standards, but from what he recalled what it lacked on the outside it made up for with plenty of love and frivolity that went on behind the simple wood doors.

The pride and joy of the Armstrong home was the massive backyard that boasted its own stream and mighty oak trees that saw many families come and go. It was where the annual Armstrong reunion was held, and if he closed his eyes he could almost see the platoon of screaming children running through the grass, aunts, uncles and cousins sitting in striped chairs, stretched out on blankets, or giving orders to the cooks about how real barbecue was supposed to be done. This was the kind of life he'd always wanted. A big family, a house filled with love and a woman whom he adored. How could Desiree have turned her back on all this for the sterile existence of the city?

It had always been like pulling teeth to get her

to come home. She found myriad reasons why she couldn't go, didn't want to go; from illness to work to being too tired.

Why? What was here that she couldn't face?

He got out of the truck and walked toward the front door, noticing that the house could use a paint job and the steps were in need of repair. He knocked and waited, listening for sounds of life from inside.

Several moments later the door inched open and Desiree's mother stood in the archway with a quizzical expression on her face.

"Yes? Can I help you?" She wiped her hands on a towel that was tucked around the waistband of her skirt.

"I don't know if you remember me, Mrs. Armstrong. I'm Lincoln Davenport."

Vera peered a bit closer at him and her hand flew to her chest. "Oh, my goodness. Lincoln." A broad smile spread across the mouth that was so much like her daughter's. "Come in. Come in." She stepped aside and Lincoln walked in.

He turned to face her as she closed the door.

"I'm sorry to just drop in on you like this without calling first."

"No problem. Can I get you something to drink?" Then suddenly she stopped. A frown creased her forehead. "Is something wrong with Desiree? Is she okay?"

He held up his hands. "Desi is fine. Really."

Her expression relaxed and her smile returned. "Then you're here visiting relatives? I don't remember

Desi ever saying you had relatives in the area." She headed for the kitchen. "Come, we'll sit and talk in the kitchen. I was putting on dinner."

Lincoln followed her and took a seat at the counter.

"Iced tea?"

"Sure. That sounds great."

She went to the fridge and took out a pitcher of iced tea, then took two glasses from the cupboard and set them on the counter.

"So what brings you all the way out here, Lincoln?" She handed him a glass of tea.

He swallowed and looked her in the eye. "Actually it's about Desiree."

Slowly she sat down, holding on to the edge of the counter as if bracing herself for something awful.

"I guess you know that Desi and I haven't…seen each other in five years."

She nodded.

"Well, this past weekend…"

He went on to tell her about how he and Desiree had reconnected, how she seemed so happy and then suddenly turned cold again. That he was worried about her and more importantly he wanted to know what she was constantly running from. That he still loved her and knew that she loved him as well but was unwilling to work out their issues.

"I know it may be out of line for me to ask you these kinds of questions about your daughter, but I need to understand. I need to know if I should try to stick it out or walk away for the last time."

Mrs. Armstrong sighed heavily and pushed herself up from the table and walked to the backyard window.

"Desiree was always the most sensitive of my three daughters. She would cry at the slightest thing, always took in stray pets, looked after anyone who was sick or injured. She has a kind and giving heart, always open and accepting."

Lincoln listened, trying to reconcile the Desiree he knew with the person her mother described. He couldn't.

"Her father pampered her. She was his favorite. He took her everywhere with him. They were inseparable. I think her sisters resented all the attention Louis paid to Desi. I talked to him about it, how it would alienate Desiree from her sisters. That it wasn't healthy. He said I was overreacting, that he loved all of his daughters, but that Desiree needed him more than the others."

"What happened? What changed her?"

She turned to face him. "It was Desiree's tenth birthday," she said, a note of wistfulness in her voice. "Louis planned a big party. It was all he could talk about. The backyard was decorated like something from a fairy tale. He hired a clown for the children. He even had a pony. Desi was so excited." She swallowed hard and lowered her head as her eyes filled. "I'm sorry." She sniffed and reached for a napkin from the holder on the counter.

"It's okay, Mrs. Armstrong, you don't have to—"
"No. No…you need to finally understand."

By the time Lincoln was back on the road, his head was spinning with all that Desiree's mother had told him. His heart ached for her. What he was told explained so much about Desiree. But now that he had some of the answers, the question still remained: how could he use this new knowledge to help Desiree become all the woman that she could be? And would she let him?

Chapter 22

"Excuse me." Desiree stepped up to the reception desk.

Terri looked up from the computer and smiled. "Well, hello. I haven't seen much of you since you arrived. Are you enjoying your stay?"

"Yes. But I need to leave. Something has come up and I have to get back to New York."

"Oh, nothing serious, I hope," Terri said, itching for details.

"Not serious but important. I need a ride into town and a train schedule."

Terri looked at her a moment to see if she could discern anything in Desiree's eyes. She saw nothing. *She'd make a good poker player,* Terri thought absently. She reached beneath the desk and pulled out several leaflets. She fished through them until she found the right one, then opened it up and turned it toward Desiree.

"There is a train leaving at three, and the last one leaves at six."

Desiree glanced above Terri's head to the clock on the wall. It was already two forty-five. She'd never make it.

"Can someone drive me to the train for the six o'clock departure?"

"I'll put a call in to Josh. He's taking over since Mr. D. went out of town."

Desiree kept her expression even. "Really? Did he say when he would be back? I mean, I'd like to say goodbye before I leave."

"He said he might be gone a few days." She rested her elbows on the counter and leaned forward. She lowered her voice to a sister-girl level. "I have his cell phone number if you really need to reach him."

Desiree shook her head and forced a smile. "No, that won't be necessary. I'll just leave him a note."

"I'm sure he wouldn't mind if I gave it to you," Terri pressed. She took a piece of paper from the desk and scribbled the number down, then handed it to Desiree. She smiled. "Just in case."

Desiree swallowed. "Thanks," she mumbled and stuck the number in the back pocket of her jeans. "I'll probably never use it."

Terri shrugged. "Probably."

"So you'll let me know if Josh can take me?"

"I'll put a call in to him now. Do you think you'll be coming back or are you totally checking out?"

"I won't be back."

Terri nodded. "Well, I hope the service was good and that your accommodations were up to par. We take a lot of pride in how our guests are treated. Mr. D. would be really upset if he thought you didn't enjoy your stay."

"Everything was fine. Really."

"Listen, I know you don't know me from Adam's house cat and you may think I'm totally out of line, but Mr. D. is a really cool guy. He gave me a job when no one else would give me the time of day. And I appreciate that. I look out for him, because he sure won't look out for himself. All he does is think of other people and this place." She waved her arm expansively.

"I don't see what that has to do with me."

"I'm getting to that part. See, ever since you got here…well, Mr. D has been like a new man. Ya know?"

"No, I don't."

"His entire expression changed when he realized it was you that was coming. I don't know what kind of relationship you have with him, but it must be special. He wanted to make sure that your every need was taken care of. He's been happier since you've come. I mean really happy. Most times he's…well, just serious, business minded. Not that he's not friendly or anything, but just hard to connect with." She looked into Desiree's eyes. "All that changed when you came. And last night when he got your note about dinner, I saw that old vacant look come back in his eyes."

Desiree's heart beat a little faster. "Why are you telling me all this?"

"So you'll know." She stared at Desiree, her mouth firm. "I'll call Josh and tell him you're leaving."

Desiree returned to her cabin and looked at her suitcases lined up by the door. Terri's words echoed in her head. She didn't want to hurt Lincoln again. He didn't deserve it. She had so many emotional issues that she needed to deal with before she could even think about having a healthy relationship. Part of her wanted to stay and try to work it out. But the reality was, she must return to New York. Rachel's message, though calm in tone, was truly anything but. Just as Rachel could read her like a book, Desiree always knew when Rae was pretending everything was cool. When she'd finally reached her in London, Rachel brought her up to date on all that was transpiring back in the city. The fire was under investigation, Carl was frantic to get in touch with her and the most frightening of all was the possibility that the fire was intentionally set.

Desiree walked out into the back and sat down on the rocks that braced the tiny creek. Why would someone want to destroy everything that she'd worked so hard to attain? She couldn't believe that, didn't want to believe it. It had to be an accident. It was the only explanation.

As much as she didn't want to have to deal with Carl at the moment, she couldn't very well leave him in the lurch after all he'd done for her. Rachel said the inspectors wanted to talk to her, as well. There wasn't much more that she could tell them. She didn't know anything.

The easy way out would be to simply stay put. Let the professionals work it out among themselves. But she'd been taking the easy way out for a long time. She'd go to New York, do what needed to be done, and then would finally come to terms about her and Lincoln. That is, if he was still interested.

The vision of her standing alone in the woods, with nothing and no one familiar around her, sprang before her eyes. She didn't want to spend the rest of her life that way. She couldn't.

The instant Desiree left the main house, Terri got on the phone and dialed Lincoln's cell phone. It rang and rang until his voice mail came on.

"Hey, Mr. D. This is Terri. It's not an emergency or anything, but it would be really cool if you called back as soon as you could. Thanks."

She hung up and leaned on the counter, tapping her long nails against the polished wood. Of course this was none of her business, but after all, Mr. D. needed to know what was happening so he could make a decision. Didn't he? She sure hoped that he would call back before she put the call in to Josh. Mr. D. would know what to do, 'cause if it was up to her, Ms. Girl wouldn't be leaving anytime soon. She smiled and waited.

Chapter 23

Lincoln kept his cell phone on vibrate during his conversation with Mrs. Armstrong. He'd felt it go off but had totally put the call out of his mind until he was back on the road. He pulled off on the side and took out the phone. He read the dial for recent incoming calls. It was from Terri. He frowned as he dialed the voice mail. What could possibly have happened in such a short period of time?

He listened to the message and debated about calling back. He'd be home in another seven hours if he didn't stop. She said it wasn't urgent. He checked the time on the dashboard clock. Four-fifteen. *Hmm.* He returned the call. Terri picked up on the first ring.

"Terri, it's me. What's up? Everything okay?"

"Not exactly, but I got a feeling you would want to know about this." She went on to tell him about her conversation with Desiree.

"Did Josh pick her up yet?"

"Nope. I can't seem to find him," she said in a tone that let him know she was lying.

He shook his head and laughed to himself. For once he was actually grateful for Terri's nosiness.

"Look, go ahead and call Josh."

"Are you sure?" she asked, surprised by his response.

"Yes, I'm sure. If you need me, I'll be in New York." Terri smiled in triumph. "Sure thing, Mr. D."

"And, Terri…"

"Yes?"

"Thanks." He hung up.

Lincoln turned on his fuzz buster and hit the gas. If he did a solid eighty miles an hour all the way back he'd make great time. Now, where would Desiree go when she returned? Her only choice, if not a hotel, was Rachel's place. He smiled. Whatever it was that they had to deal with, this time they would deal with it together, whether Desiree liked it or not.

Desiree barely made the train. She'd run through the station with just enough time to get on board before the doors closed. She'd have to pay the extra money for buying her ticket on the train. If she didn't know better she'd swear that Terri wanted her to miss her train. And Josh wasn't much better. He seemed to relish taking her along the scenic route and pointing out every nook and cranny that they passed.

Breathing heavily, she finally found a window seat, stowed her baggage on the rack above her head and sat down.

Now that she was actually on the train she had a moment to think. What was really going on? But she couldn't imagine what additional information she could give to Carl, or anyone else for that matter. He must be pretty desperate to pay a visit to Rachel.

She leaned back in the seat and stared out the window. That night was still clear in her mind. She'd gone over what had happened hundreds of times. Still she could not come up with one clear bit of information to explain what transpired. She certainly didn't have any idea of who would want to intentionally set the building on fire. The mere idea made her shiver.

She folded her arms and closed her eyes. She was returning to New York, still homeless, and if she didn't find some solid means of employment, she'd be penniless, as well. Her teaching job only paid enough to put a couple of meals on the table and keep her bank account from dipping below the cutoff point. It certainly wasn't enough to live on, pay rent and keep up the insurance on her car.

At least she still had her Mustang—her pride and joy. But she'd probably sell it if things really got bad.

How could she have allowed herself to get into this position? Her entire existence hinged on the gallery and

Carl Hampton. She'd never permitted herself to be that dependent on anyone. That was her first and last mistake of that kind. She was going to get her act together. Find a way to pay Carl back and move on with her life.

She thought of the easel and paints that she'd reluctantly packed and brought along with her. Maybe in time she would actually pull them out and use them again.

The train pulled into its first stop and a new crew of passengers got on. Desiree opened her eyes and looked around at everyone searching for seats. She moved her jacket off of her lap and onto the vacant seat next to her. Maybe if she was lucky she wouldn't acquire a riding partner for the balance of the trip. She closed her eyes again and feigned sleep.

"Sorry to disturb you. But is this seat taken?"

Inwardly Desiree groaned. She opened her eyes and looked up. Recognition settled in. "Allison. Allison Wakefield, is that you?"

The woman shifted her oversized straw bag from one arm to the other and focused on Desiree.

"Desiree! Desiree Armstrong!" A smile beamed across her face. "I don't believe it."

Allison, Rachel, Carly and Desiree had all pledged to the same sorority, the Alpha Deltas, while they attended Howard University in Washington, D.C. They'd been fast friends during their college years, all of them competitive and creative. Although they'd vowed to stay connected on graduation day, many lost contact over the years, moving on with their lives and careers and to different parts of the country. Although Desiree regularly received the sorority's newsletter and invitation to attend reunions, she never submitted any information on her life and had yet to attend an event. A fact that Rachel berated her about on a regular basis.

Desiree snatched up her jacket. "Sit down. How are you? How long has it been?"

"At least eight years." Allison sat down. She lifted her head, placing her index finger on her lip and thought for a moment, then turned to Desiree. "The last time I saw you was at an art gallery in Washington. It was a benefit exhibit, if I remember correctly. What have you been up to since then?"

"Trying to be an artist," she said and laughed lightly.

Allison patted Desiree's arm. "Trying! Girl, pleeze. From what I remember, you had more talent than you knew what to do with." She settled herself in the seat and placed her bag on the floor between her feet. Allison lowered her voice and turned sympathetic eyes on Desiree. "I read about the fire. I'm so sorry. When I saw the article I couldn't believe it was you. But it was, wasn't it? I was just talking to Carly about it a week or so ago when I went to visit her in Martha's Vineyard. I'm terribly sorry, Desiree."

Desiree lowered her head and nodded. "Thanks."

They were quiet for a moment.

"Have you seen any of the other sorors?" Allison asked, breaking the uncomfortable silence. "I've been so bad about keeping up with everyone. Except for Carly. We talk occasionally."

"You and me both." They laughed. "I stay in touch with Rachel Givens. You remember her, right?"

"Yes, yes." She frowned for another moment in thought, then brightened. "She was into jewelry or something, right?"

"Yes, she actually has her own business. Honey Child Accessories."

Allison chuckled. "Sounds like a name Rachel would pick. So where are you heading to or coming from?"

"I was out at Sag Harbor for a few days, but I'm heading back to New York."

"So am I. I was planning on being in the city for a few days visiting friends and shopping. Maybe we could have lunch or something."

Desiree briefly glanced at Allison's elegant attire, the diamonds that flashed on her finger and in her ears, and knew that she would be hard-pressed to make herself presentable enough to hang with the likes of Allison. Especially with her money being as tight as it was.

She forced a smile. "Sounds good. I know I'm going to be swamped this week, but I'll sure try."

"Great." Allison reached down and picked up her bag, then dug inside and pulled out her wallet. She plucked out a business card and jotted a number on the back, then handed it to Desiree. "Call me anytime. You can always leave a message."

"Thanks." Desiree tucked the card into the top

pocket of her denim shirt. "So what have you been up to? You look to be doing well for yourself."

Allison smiled. "I recently got married." She flashed her ring. "My husband was initially the subject of an investigative story that I was working on. One thing led to another and…"

"Well, congratulations. Who is the lucky man?"

"Jacob Covington."

"*The* Jacob Covington?"

Allison grinned with pride. "One and the same."

"His book has been on the bestseller list for months."

"He's working on another one. We hope it will do just as well."

Desiree was thoughtful for a moment. "You said you met him as part of an investigative story?"

"Yes, I'm an investigative journalist."

"No kidding. That must be exciting. But you said you just got married and you're on the road already?"

"Actually, the reason for my trip to New York is a bit more…complicated than just visiting friends," she confided. "I know it's been a while since we've seen or spoken with each other, but I always felt we kind of had a bond, you and I, more so than some of the others." Her gregarious expression turned serious, her eyes intent. She lowered her voice. "Anyway, with us being 'sisters'…I really need someone to talk to and I know that it will never get past you."

Desiree arched a brow in interest and turned slightly in her seat to face Allison. "Of course not."

"My newspaper has been sending me all over the country to investigate alleged insurance frauds. It's killing the industry and the consumer. I have some people I need to interview and…"

While Desiree listened to Allison her mind was working, too. Allison could be just the person she needed.

Chapter 24

Lincoln hit I-95 North and from there he knew it would be clear sailing. He'd connected his cell phone to the car charger and had it hooked up to his OnStar system. He spoke in the direction of the phone.

"Call The Port."

The automatic dial rang the inn and moments later Terri was on the line.

"Hey, Mr. D. Everything okay?"

"Fine. Listen, did Josh get Desiree to the train in time?"

"Yes, she made it. Just barely."

"Okay. Thanks. What time does it get into Penn Station?"

"Hmm. Hang on, let me check the schedule."

He could hear her fumbling with papers and then a guest walked in. She had a lengthy conversation with a woman about extra towels before getting back to him.

"Sorry about that. The train should get in around eight. Give or take a few minutes."

"Thanks. Did she mention if someone was going to meet her?"

He heard her snap her fingers.

"Wow, why didn't I think of that? Sorry, Mr. D., I didn't ask."

"Not a problem."

"Hey, Mr. D....I know I may be out of line for asking this but...what's the real story with you and Ms. Armstrong? She seems like a really nice woman...a little distant but nice...and I got the impression that she really likes you. She just doesn't know what to do about it."

Lincoln shook his head, flabbergasted by her boldness. But he shouldn't be. When he hired Terri, he knew her background. She was a twenty-two-year-old single mom, with little education, struggling to take care of her son and herself. She had a lot of street smarts and plenty of street ways. And she might be a bit rough around the edges, but she had a heart of gold and was a great worker. He never had a worry when he left her in charge, and her loyalty to him was her way of saying thanks. That much he knew.

"You think you can keep a secret, Terri?"

"Of course!" She almost sounded indignant.

"Well, Desi and I go way back. I'm hoping that we can go way forward. Know what I mean?"

He could hear her laughter.

"Yeah, I know what you mean. And if there's anything I can do to help—just holla! Personally, if it was up to me—which it wasn't—I wouldn't have let her get on the train in the first place. Nothing like getting stuff straight on your own turf. Know what I mean?"

Lincoln chuckled. "Yeah, I know what you mean. Anyway, I'll check back in when I arrive in New York."

"Take her some flowers, Mr. D, women like her love flowers."

"I'll keep that in mind. Take care."

"Later, Mr. D."

Chapter 25

Desiree and Allison disembarked at New York's Pennsylvania Station and wound their way through the crowd to the cab stand exit on 7th Avenue.

"Can I give you a lift somewhere?" Allison asked.

"If you don't mind, you can drop me off at Rachel's place."

"Sure, not a problem. Listen, I know this may not be any of my business, but do you have a place to stay? I mean…"

"I'm going to be staying at Rachel's for a while until I can get relocated. She's out of town for a few weeks and said I can use her place."

"Well, my door is always open. Don't hesitate to ask. If there's anything you need, just let me know."

"As a matter of fact, after listening to your story about your current assignment, I was wondering if you might be willing to look into something for me, as well."

Allison arched a brow. "Sure. What is it?"

"There seems to be some questions about how the fire started. There is some concern about arson."

"Arson! Oh, my goodness."

Desiree nodded her head and went on to tell her about all that Rachel had relayed to her.

"That's part of the reason why I came back."

"I see. And this Carl Hampton, how much did you know about him before you signed on?"

"Not much, I'm afraid to say. I was so flattered and broke. I'll never make that mistake again."

"Hmm." Allison was thoughtful for a moment. "The first thing I would do is to start getting some background on Mr. Hampton. You have no idea how many people sabotage their own property to get the insurance money. He may not have done it himself but he certainly could have had it done," she added, her journalistic instincts kicking in. "First thing tomorrow, I'll start making some calls."

Desiree opened the door of the next available taxi. "Thanks, Allison."

Allison stepped inside the cab and Desiree got in beside her. "That's what sorors are for."

Once settled in the cab, Allison whipped out her ever-ready notebook and a pen. "Do you have a phone number and business address for Hampton, and what about your assistant…Cynthia? I'll need her information, too."

Desiree took out her electronic organizer and scrolled through the information until she found Carl's and Cynthia's.

"Can I ask you a question?"

"Sure," Allison said as she took down the information.

"Why do you need Cynthia's information? You don't think she's involved?"

"No one is above suspicion, Desiree. That's the first thing you learn in this business. As a matter of fact I may give Carly's husband, Jackson, a call if I hit any roadblocks."

"Carly's husband?"

"Oh, didn't I mention that he's a private investigator? And a good one, too." She smiled and patted Desiree's thigh. "We'll get to the bottom of it. Hopefully it is as it appears—an accident. But if it's not we'll find that out, too."

Suddenly Desiree's simple inquiry was taking a dark turn. A shiver ran through her.

Lincoln checked the time on the dash. Desiree's train, if it was on time, should have arrived hours earlier. He'd just reached the Holland Tunnel and would be in Manhattan in a matter of minutes. A short hop across town and he should pull up in front of Rachel's place in another hour.

He laughed to himself. His entire day had been totally on the spur of the moment. Fortunately, so far it had turned out for the best. He hoped the rest of his trip would follow suit.

He had no idea what Desiree would do when she saw him, if she would even let him in. But one thing he was certain of, he was not going back to Sag Harbor until they talked, really talked, and she gave him the answers that he needed.

He exited the Holland Tunnel and headed uptown. He'd know soon enough.

"Thanks for the lift," Desiree said, taking her suitcase from the trunk of the cab.

"Anytime." Allison looked up at Rachel's building. "Looks like Rachel has done okay for herself, too."

"That she has. Her business is booming, but it takes her out of town quite a bit. Hopefully we can all get together at some point."

"I'd really like that. Let's plan on it. I'd love for you to meet Jacob."

"Well, I don't want to hold you."

"Yeah, I should be getting in. I have a big day tomorrow. I'll call you and keep you posted on what I find out."

"Thanks."

"And remember, if you change your mind and get lonely in this big old house, you can always crash at my place."

"I'll definitely keep that in mind."

Allison reached over and hugged Desiree. "Everything is going to work out fine," she said, sensing Desiree's apprehension. "Trust me on that."

Desiree pressed her lips together and nodded.

Allison got back into the cab and it sped off.

For several moments, Desiree stood on the curb watching the cab until it turned the corner and disappeared. *Life is so funny,* she thought, picking up her suitcase. First, of all the places to rest her head she wound up at the one owned by her ex-fiancé. Then, during an impromptu train ride, she ran into an old college friend who happened to be an investigative journalist. She supposed that the old saying "your past will always catch up with you" was true.

She turned and walked up the steps to the front door of Rachel's building. If that old saying was true, what else from her past would come back for a visit?

Chapter 26

Cynthia stepped out of the taxi on Park Avenue and 72nd Street. She looked up at the ornate apartment complex that housed many of New York's who's who from rock stars to corporate moguls. The historic building had been the venue for many movies and television programs and it was said to hold long-buried secrets from starlets and politicians who used it for their rendezvous. Cynthia had spent her teen years there, living the privileged life of the wealthy, attending the best schools, meeting the right people. But it was never a life that she aspired to. Unfortunately, it was the bone of contention between her and her mother, one that had severely severed their mother-daughter relationship.

Her mother could never fathom how *her* daughter

could walk away from all that she'd provided for her to live the life she chose to live. And she'd done everything in her power to change that. Including seeing to it that the one person that Cynthia had ever loved was permanently removed from her life. To this day she had not forgiven her mother for that ultimate betrayal and never would.

She walked to the front door and was greeted by Jefferson, the doorman, who had been opening doors for Cynthia for as long as she could remember.

"Ms. Hastings, so good to see you." He tipped his hat.

"Good to see you, too, Jefferson. How have you been?"

"Can't complain. Going to visit your mother?"

"Yes."

"You're a good daughter. So many children forget all about their parents when they move on with their lives. But not you." He smiled. "And I know she appreciates it, too, especially with her not being well. You're all she ever talks about."

Cynthia's monthly visits were purely out of a sense of duty, not love, and she wanted to get it over as quickly as possible. She made a show of checking her watch, hoping that Jefferson would get the hint; otherwise he could very well talk to her indefinitely and think nothing of it.

"Let me let you go. You have to excuse an old man.

Nothing like talking to a beautiful young woman to brighten the day."

Cynthia smiled wanly. "You take care, Jefferson." She walked to the elevator.

"Tell your mother I said hello."

"I sure will." She pressed the button and the doors slid open.

"What floor, ma'am?" the attendant asked.

"Thirty-three, please." She stepped inside, turned and waved at Jefferson just as the doors whooshed closed.

This was one of the few buildings left in the city that still boasted an elevator attendant. Even with all the modern conveniences, it still maintained that old-world flavor. Cynthia had to admit it was a nice touch.

"Thirty-three," the attendant announced.

"Thank you." Cynthia reached in her purse, took out two single dollars and pressed them into his gloved hand and walked out.

The heels of her Feragamo lizard pumps sank into the plush cream-colored carpet in the hallway. She took a quick look at herself in one of the gilded mirrors that hung on the wall above a Queen Anne table.

She adjusted her black Caroline Herrera jacket and checked to make sure that the crease in her matching slacks was razor sharp. The simple platinum chain hung precisely in the center of her bare chest as she opted not to wear a blouse. And her Prada handbag was the perfect complement to her shoes.

Cynthia took a deep, cleansing breath. Even now, at the age of thirty, her mother had a way of making her feel like a child. She knew that she would give a personal inspection to every iota of clothing that Cynthia had on, and she wanted her attire to at least be the one thing she and her mother didn't argue about today.

Satisfied that she'd done all she could short of morphing into someone else, she continued down the hallway and rang the bell to apartment 3300. She flipped her long blond hair over her shoulders and waited, when her heart suddenly knocked hard in her chest. She'd forgotten her earrings.

Her mind raced. She generally kept a spare pair of clip-ons in her purse. She snapped the lock open, hoping to dig them out before the door opened. If there was any justice in the world, Cynthia thought frantically, maybe Mary the housekeeper would answer and not her mother.

No such luck.

"Cynthia. I knew it was you." Her mother beamed.

As always, her mother was impeccably dressed as if she were preparing for a cover shoot. Every strand of her silver hair was in place and her jewelry gleamed from her ears, neck and wrist.

"Come in, sweetheart. Mary is in the kitchen fixing a late supper." Her all-seeing eyes quickly took in her daughter. "I see you forgot your earrings again. What happened to the diamond studs I bought you for Christmas? I don't understand how you can't keep up with your things and make yourself presentable when you come out in public. Presentation is everything. If I taught you nothing else I taught you that."

Cynthia smiled weakly. "Hello, Mother." Her stomach churned. She never seemed to remember how much she hated this place or hated her mother until she walked through the doors.

"I was in the sitting room," her mother said in a huff, still miffed about the missing earrings.

Cynthia followed her mother into what she called "the sitting room." By the average person's standard it would be considered a one-bedroom apartment. Everything about her mother was big, lavish, larger than life and utterly unnecessary. But you could never tell her mother that.

"Sit down, darling, and tell me what has been going on in your life. I was just watching the news and the most horrific things are happening in the world. It's all quite awful, one scandal after another. Not to mention terrorists on every street corner, budget deficits, orange alerts, hoodlums infiltrating every neighborhood." She began to fan herself with her ever-ready handkerchief and continued to ramble on.

She was working herself up into a state, Cynthia quickly realized, while also understanding that her mother was truly uninterested in her daughter's life. She loved to hear herself talk too much to pay even a modicum of attention to anyone else. It had always been that way. Everyone else put up with it; Cynthia moved out.

Mercifully, Mary entered the room and announced that supper was ready. In their usual ritual they moved to the dining room.

"How are you making out since that awful fire?" Cynthia's mother questioned as she shook out a linen napkin and placed it on her lap. "I suppose you'll be looking for another job." She said the last word as if it were something she could accidentally catch, like a disease. "I didn't spend all that money on your education, sending you to Europe to study, to work for someone else for the rest of your life," she went on in disgust.

She raised her salad fork and pointed it at Cynthia. "You know I could simply make a phone call and you could easily be a curator at the National Museum or the Smithsonian or open your own gallery—a real one," she sniffed.

"I was perfectly happy doing what I was doing, Mother. Something you fail to understand."

"You're right. I don't. You take up this bohemian life, work in the worst section of the city." She began fanning herself again. "That's not the life I envisioned for you, Cynthia. Not at all."

"It seems I've never lived up to any of your expectations, Mother. But I've gotten used to it by now."

Her mother flushed a crimson red. "How can someone of your upbringing become accustomed to mediocrity?" She was appalled. "Your father would roll over in his grave if he could see how you turned out."

Cynthia stood up so abruptly she knocked over her chair in the process. "Daddy was the only one who understood me, who listened, who gave a damn about what I wanted."

"I will not have you using foul language in my home." She slammed her palm down on the table, rattling the china. "Is that what that…that woman teaches you in that hellhole she calls a gallery?"

Cynthia jerked back as if slapped. Her chest heaved as if she couldn't catch her breath. "Don't you dare talk about Desiree that way. She's one of the most decent human beings I know. And she lost everything she'd worked for." She tossed her napkin on the table. "But you wouldn't know anything about that, Mother, since everything in your life has been handed to you on one of your fucking silver platters!" She picked up a dish and tossed it across the room.

Her mother let out such a gasp that Cynthia was certain she was going to have that heart attack she'd been threatening to have for years.

Mary came rushing in. "Is everything all right?" She looked from one outraged face to the other.

"No. Everything is not all right. And never has been," Cynthia uttered. She tossed her mother a final scathing look. "Enjoy your meal." With that she grabbed her purse and rushed out of the room before the tears that threatened to overflow betrayed her in front of the one person she vowed never to cry in front of again.

"You'll need me," her mother yelled out. "I know you will. You'll come back." Her voice broke. "You'll come back."

Cynthia ran to the door, bumping into the circular side table and knocking over the little statue that sat on its center. Through sheer force of habit she bent and picked it up, put it back in its place and ran out.

Once on the other side of the door, she leaned against the wall. She was shaking all over. Slowly she pulled herself together and continued down the hall, silently vowing as always that she would not come back.

But she knew she would. That agonized her more than anything.

Chapter 27

Desiree let herself in with the extra key she always kept on her key ring. As soon as she turned on the lights she was surprised to find a huge bouquet of flowers waiting to greet her. She walked over to the table and picked up the card that was tucked in the folds of red, yellow and peach roses.

Just thought I'd send a little something to brighten your day. Make yourself at home and call if you need anything. I can be there on the next flight. Hugs, Rachel.

Desiree slowly shook her head and smiled. Rachel was the best. She must have gotten her assistant to bring them over. And Rachel was right, it was just what she needed.

She took her bags to the back bedroom, intent on settling down. First thing in the morning she was going to get in touch with Carl and find out what was going on. To be truthful she certainly could understand why he was upset. She shouldn't have run off like that without a word. But that's why she was back, to make amends and find out the truth.

Desiree took off her blouse, emptied her pockets and placed Allison's business card on the dresser. She looked at the card. Hopefully Allison's investigation would turn up nothing out of the ordinary. But what if it did?

She sat down on the side of the bed. Arson was such an ugly idea to try to wrap her mind around. Who could possibly benefit by setting the gallery on fire and nearly killing her in the process? She leaned over and untied her sneakers, placing them by the side of the bed. It didn't make sense that it would be Carl. He'd invested too much. She couldn't see that he would have more to gain by destroying the place than by letting her finish her work and have the exhibit. It was all he talked about.

She stood and unzipped her jeans, stepped out of them and tossed them on the bed. It wasn't as if she had a huge staff of disgruntled employees that would try to get back at her, she thought. That didn't leave many other alternatives. Unfastening her bra, she opened her suitcase and took out her robe. She slipped her robe on and walked into the bathroom. The bottom line was, she thought, turning on the shower, the most likely suspect, if anyone, was *her*.

She'd been overworked and exhausted for weeks and must have inadvertently done something that caused the sparks that started the fire. That was the only scenario that made sense, as awful as it was. She stuck her hand under the water to test the temperature just as the doorbell rang.

Desiree fastened the belt on her robe. "Who in the world could that be?" she mumbled as she walked toward the door. "It has to be one of Rachel's eccentric clients."

She took a look through the peephole and was stunned to see who was on the other side. With some trepidation she turned the locks. She inched the door open and stuck out her head.

"Carl. What are you doing here?"

"I've been hoping you'd finally come back," he said. "I've, uh…been sitting outside. I saw you when you came in."

"You've been watching the house?" she asked, her voice hitching up a notch.

Carl held up his hand. "Not the way you think, Desiree. We need to talk." He paused. "Can I come in? Just for a minute."

Desiree looked over her shoulder as if some unseen force held the answer. She tugged in a deep breath.

"All right." She unhooked the latch and opened the door. "Come in." She stepped aside and let him in, then closed the door behind him.

She turned to face him and hugged her arms around her body, realizing that she had nothing on beneath her robe. She crossed to the far side of the room.

"First, I want to apologize for not coming to see you in the hospital. It's just that—"

"There's no need to apologize, Carl. If I didn't want to be there, I'm sure others didn't, either." She tried to laugh.

He lowered his head and nodded, then looked up at her. "Things are really out of control, Desiree. I'm up to the top of my head with investigators, investors." He began to pace, then stopped and turned to her. "And I have nothing to tell them."

Slowly Desiree sat down on an overstuffed chair. "I know I owe you a great deal, Carl, and whatever I need to do to make it up to you I will, no matter how long it takes."

He suddenly walked toward her. "What I need from you is for you to start painting. We have barely two months before the exhibit is to launch. If I can at least tell the investors that you are prepared to go through with it, some of the pressure will be taken off me."

Desiree swallowed hard. Her hand went to her throat. "I…I've tried…I haven't been able to do anything." She looked up at him, hoping that he would understand.

"But you have to! Too much is riding on this. You owe me more than some excuse about how you can't!"

"You don't understand."

"No, I don't. And I'm not going to sit idly by while you ruin me."

"Ruin you!" She stood, her robe slightly parting. "You came to me. You offered me the chance of a lifetime, and like a fool I went for it. I don't know what all you are involved in. You convinced me it was your money, your dream. And now it's about investors and other people's money."

He came toward her, his blue eyes darkening. "That's right, Desiree," he said in a low voice. "Other people's money. People who aren't as benevolent as I am. People who won't take 'I can't' as an excuse." Suddenly he grabbed her by the arms and pulled her hard against him. He looked down into her startled eyes. "You can make this all go away." His gaze raked over her, dipping down into the opening of her robe. His thumbs grazed her nipples.

"Carl! Let me go."

"Desiree…"

He pressed harder against her, locking his arm around her waist.

She struggled to get free. "Carl! No!"

"Don't you know how long I've wanted you? Do you really think I did all that I've done for you because you were so incredibly talented?" He slid his free hand in between the folds of her robe and stroked her thighs.

"Desiree…please…let me love you. I can take care of you…." He lowered his head to kiss her while his hand continued to explore her thigh, easing up to her hip.

Desiree whipped her head back and forth as she struggled against him until she remembered an old high school defensive tactic.

An instant later Carl hollered as if he'd been stabbed and doubled over in agony. Desiree instantly backed up. "Get out! Get out!" She ran for the phone.

Carl stumbled after her, grabbed the back of her robe and pushed her to the floor, pinning her beneath him.

She screamed even as he tried to get his hand to cover her mouth.

"Shh. I'm not going to hurt you," he whispered hotly in her ear. He pushed up her robe.

"Oh, God, no. Carl, please. No!"

The door suddenly burst open and before she realized what was happening Carl was tossed off of her. She crawled away on her hands and knees and turned to see Lincoln beating Carl mercilessly.

They rolled around on the floor until Lincoln virtually lifted Carl off the floor by his lapels and herded him to the door, pushing him out on the other side and locking the door behind him. He rushed over to Desiree and knelt beside her.

"Baby, are you okay?" His eyes rolled over her, looking for any sign of injury.

"Yes…I think so," she said in a shaky voice.

Lincoln gathered her in his arms and held her tenderly against him. "If anything would have happened…" He couldn't finish the thought. He kissed the top of her head and held her for what seemed like hours until she stopped shaking.

"H-how did you know?" she finally asked in a shaky voice.

"I called The Port and Terri told me you left. I knew you would come here. When I came up to the door and heard you screaming…" He stroked her hair.

"I never should have let him in. But I didn't think…" A tremor ran through her.

"We need to call the police and report this." He helped her to her feet and walked her to the couch. He picked up the phone.

"No. I'm fine. He won't be back. And he won't try anything like that again." She tugged her robe tighter.

"Desi, you can't let him get away with this."

"Oh, he won't. Just the idea that at any moment the police will come knocking on his door will be enough to keep him in line." She looked at Lincoln with determination in her eyes. "I don't need Carl locked up and me on the stand testifying for an attempted rape. I need him out on the street doing whatever it is that he does so that we can get to the bottom of the fire."

Reluctantly, he hung up the phone. "I don't agree. I think the bastard needs to be put under the jailhouse." He crossed the room and stood in front of her. "But this is the deal and I'm not taking no for an answer.

You don't call the police and have him locked up, then I don't leave your side. Simple as that. Now take it or leave it."

Desiree tugged on her bottom lip with her teeth. She'd seen that look in Lincoln's eyes and she knew it would be pointless to argue.

"All right," she conceded.

"Now, we can either stay here or we can stay at my place uptown. Your call. But I'm not leaving you alone. And that's my call."

So this is what it's like to have a dark knight in shining armor come to your rescue.

"Let me put on some clothes and repack my bag," she said, looking him square in the eye.

Chapter 28

Carl was livid and humiliated. He sat in his car unable to move. How could he have allowed himself to do something like that? He slammed his palm against the steering wheel. What had gotten into him? It wasn't in his nature to be violent, especially toward women. But something inside him had snapped.

What must Desiree be thinking? Had he hurt her? He glanced up at the window. Her lights were still on and that man, whoever he was, remained inside. He clenched his jaw. Who was he and what was his relationship to Desiree? The time to worry about that was not now. At any moment he was certain the police were going to pull up. How could he have been so stupid?

Taking one last look up at the window, he finally put the car in gear and drove off.

Several times on his way home, he thought about going back and apologizing. But he felt certain that Desiree wouldn't listen to anything he said. When he pulled onto his street, it suddenly dawned on him that his home would be the first place the police would look for him. He kept going. Until he could make peace with Desiree, he'd have to lie low at least for a little while.

Hours later, Cynthia was still shaken by her visit with her mother. Even after all these years her mother still had the power to make her fall apart. She'd killed her father as sure as if she'd personally given him the heart attack that took his life, and she ran off her second husband. Now all she had left was her money, her housekeeper and Cynthia.

Cynthia turned on the light in the kitchen and opened the fridge and gazed at the scanty contents. The strongest thing she had in the house was apple juice. What she really needed was a drink. With that determination in mind, she returned to her bedroom, picked up her jacket and her purse and headed out. She needed anonymity—to be in a place where no one knew her and she didn't know them. She snatched up her keys from the table in the hall and headed out.

Twenty minutes later she pulled up in front of a nondescript bar/lounge. She parked her car and got out.

The interior was typically dim, which suited her just

fine. There were only a few patrons, most of whom were totally involved in staring down at the bottom of their glasses. She found an empty table in the back of the room and sat down.

"What can I getcha?" a girl who didn't look old enough to babysit asked her.

"Gin and tonic with a twist."

"Coming right up." She smacked her wad of gum and switched away, her black micromini not leaving much to the imagination.

Cynthia looked around, her eyes slowly adjusting to the almost nonexistent light. She'd been reduced to this, she thought. The waitress returned with her drink, and before she could set it down, Cynthia took it. She closed her eyes as the liquor slid down her throat. The young waitress gave her a look and walked away. Cynthia didn't care. She stirred her drink and took another long swallow.

All she'd ever wanted in life was her own life, she thought, misery rising in her belly like the smell of sour milk. Her mother had refused to give it to her. Even after she moved away, her mother still tried to control her life. She finished off her drink and signaled for another one.

"Mind if I join you?"

Cynthia looked up. The face of an unfamiliar man stood above her. He wasn't bad to look at. What harm could it do?

"Not at all, have a seat."

The waitress returned with her drink. "What can I get for you, sir?"

"Jack Daniel's, no ice."

"Right away." She gave him an extra smile.

"What is a pretty lady like you doing here alone?"

"It would take more time than you have," she said in a monotone. She tossed back half of her drink and set it down.

"Can't be that bad."

"Says who?"

He chuckled. "At least you still have your sense of humor."

"A matter of perspective." She finished off her drink and ordered another when the waitress returned with the Jack Daniel's for the somewhat handsome stranger.

"Cheers," he said, raising his glass.

Numbly, Cynthia tapped her empty glass against his.

"My name is Lance Freeman."

"That's nice." She nodded her thanks to the waitress and took a good gulp. The edges of her life were getting soft and fuzzy.

"Do you have a name?"

"Of course. What a silly question." She giggled.

"Maybe you should slow down."

"Maybe you should bug off," she tossed back, her tone turning nasty.

Lance leaned back and looked at Cynthia. She was beautiful, intelligent, he assumed, well-off from the cut of her clothes, and obviously very hurt and lonely.

"I'm a pretty good listener."

She looked at him through bleary eyes. "What if I don't want to talk?"

"I think you do."

She snorted. "What makes you so smart?"

"I listen to people for a living."

She squinted and tried to get him in focus. "What does that mean? You some kinda shrink?" She giggled.

"So I've heard."

Cynthia laughed. "You're funny and kinda cute, too." She reached for her glass and Lance put a hand on top of hers to stop her.

"Why don't I get you a cup of coffee?"

"I really want to get drunk, you know," she said, struggling to get the words across her tongue.

"That's pretty obvious, but why?"

"'Cause I hate her and she makes me hate myself," she slurred.

"That's pretty tough. But this doesn't help," he said, pointing to her glass.

She shrugged. "Got a better idea?"

"You could start with your name."

"Cynthia. My friends call me Cynthia." She giggled.

"Well, Cynthia, why don't I see that you get home safely? Did you drive?"

She nodded and the room spun.

"Not a good idea for you to be driving. Where is your car?"

She shrugged. "It should be outside."

Lance stood up and pulled out his wallet. He put three twenties on the table, then helped Cynthia to her feet. "Do you remember the color of your car?"

"Red!" she said, her face lighting up like a child who gets the right answer in class.

"Okay. Come on."

He put his arm around her waist, tucked her purse under her arm, then ushered her outside. The cool night air slightly cleared her head.

"I feel…like…a fool," she mumbled, leaning against him.

"It happens to the best of us. Do you have any idea where you parked your car?"

Cynthia stopped walking and blinked several times to clear her head. She looked up and down the street until she spotted her car. "Over there," she said, pointing to her car.

Lance walked her to the passenger door. "Give me your keys."

Cynthia fumbled in her purse and dug out her car keys.

Lance opened the door and helped her inside, then came around to the driver's side and got in behind the wheel.

"Address?" He turned the key in the ignition.

Cynthia took a deep breath and told him.

"Sit back and relax. I'll have you home in no time."

Cynthia leaned her head back and closed her eyes. "Why are you doing this?"

"What, treating you decent?"

"Yes."

"Maybe because I'm a decent guy." He glanced at her, then back at the street.

"You could be a serial killer," she muttered.

"Yeah, I could be."

"I hope not," she muttered and drifted off.

Shortly after, Lance pulled to a stop in front of Cynthia's building. He lightly tapped her shoulder. She mumbled something under her breath and snuggled deeper into the plush seat.

Lance was thoughtful for a moment. Without any options he got out of the car and came around to her side. He plucked her purse from beneath her hip and looked for her ID. At least if he knew what her last name was he would know which apartment to put her in. He found a piece of mail.

"Okay, pretty lady, let's go." He gathered her in his arms and lifted her out of the car. She curved her body against his and tucked her head on his neck. Lance smiled.

Juggling the weight of a half-asleep Cynthia and trying to get her door open without dropping her wasn't easy, but he managed. When he finally got the door open and turned on the light he was pleasantly surprised by the tasteful and obviously expensive surroundings. The lady had class, even if she was a little troubled. He looked down into her sleeping face and wondered what had really happened to make her do what she'd done to herself—get so out of her head that she would let a perfect stranger drive her car and take her home.

She was right, if he'd been a different type of man, she would be easy prey. But what he really wanted to do was get to know this sleeping beauty under better circumstances.

Lance found her bedroom and placed her down gently on the fluffy rose-colored comforter. He took off her shoes and covered her up with her robe that was draped across the foot of the bed. He put her purse and car keys on the dresser, then dug in his jacket pocket for a pen and paper. He wrote a quick note and included his phone number. Hopefully he'd hear from her again.

Taking a final look, he closed her bedroom door and left. As he walked to the corner to hail a cab, the image and feel of Cynthia in his arms wouldn't leave him. What he'd done tonight he'd never done in his life, but there was something about her that touched him in a place that had been dark and vacant for a very long time. He hoped she'd call, but if she didn't he knew where to find her.

Chapter 29

Lincoln opened the door to his Upper East Side apartment and stepped aside to let Desiree in.

"Make yourself at home," he said, switching on the lights. He put her bag down in the foyer.

Slowly, Desiree walked inside and took a look around. The space was totally Lincoln: stylish, classy and thoroughly a man's space. The living room was done in a soft chocolate brown, the leather couch and love seat looked good enough to eat. African-print throws were the only accessories other than the smoked-glass coffee and end tables.

What was most striking was that on the stark white walls hung one of her original paintings, the one she'd painted for him years earlier. It was a picture of a white sandy beach with a lone house just off the shore set against brilliant blue water and soft clouds.

She turned to him. "You kept it."

"Yeah," he said simply. "It was the inspiration for The Port."

"I don't know what to say…"

"Your paintings have more power than you realize." He quickly changed topics when he saw the pain leap back into her eyes. "Let me show you your room so you can get settled." He led her down a narrow hallway to the spare bedroom and opened the door. "It's not much but it's comfortable." He turned on the light. "I use it for my office sometimes when I stay over in the city."

The room was fully equipped with the latest in technology, from a state-of-the-art computer system complete with speakers, to a fax machine and scanner, a television and a queen-size bed.

"I'll get you some clean linen and towels."

"I can do it. Just show me where."

"The linen closet is right next to the bathroom. Take whatever you need. I'll get your bag."

Desiree followed him out, then peeked down the hall toward what she figured was the bathroom but found his bedroom instead. Tentatively she pushed the partially opened door and looked inside. In her mind's eye she could see her and Lincoln sharing many nights in the comfort of the bed that dominated the room.

She jumped at the movement behind her.

"I promise to stay out of your room during the night,"

he said with a smile that crinkled his eyes. He braced his hand against the door frame. "Are you okay?"

The tenderness in his voice moved her heart. She nodded, afraid to speak.

"Let me show you the rest of the place." He put her bag in her room and took her on a tour, showing her where to find things in the kitchen, and extra blankets in a spare closet. He took her downstairs to a huge room that had been converted into a workout center. It had every piece of exercise equipment imaginable. The room was a three-dimensional infomercial. No wonder he was in such great shape, Desiree thought. Then he took her to his prized workroom in the attic space.

"This is where I do all the designing for the buildings," he said with a note of pride.

Desiree stepped into the space that was filled with the tools of his trade: a drafting table, gooseneck lamp, another computer, filing cabinets and a wall filled with designs.

She turned to him. "I never knew you designed," she said, surprised by the obvious talent. She took a closer look at the sketches.

"I don't…not really." He shrugged. "I kind of fool around. I took a couple of design classes just so that I would be able to get my ideas across."

"I'm impressed."

If he could blush he would have. "That means a lot coming from you."

"It's true, Lincoln." She stepped close to him and

looked into his eyes. "You were always talented. And you found a way to express it. It's a gift."

"Like yours?"

She turned away. "We're not talking about me."

"When will we talk about you, Desi? You can't stay in hibernation forever. That's why I brought you the easel and the paints. Art is in your blood, it's like breathing to you. How long do you think you can go without it?"

She wrapped her arms around her body. "I've tried, Lincoln. I just need some time, that's all."

"But you seemed…happy with the gifts. Was that all an act?"

She took a breath. "I…I didn't want to disappoint you."

"I see."

"No. I don't think you do, Lincoln. You weren't in that room that night. You don't know what it's like to be so terrified that you can't breathe, can't sleep, are afraid of the dark, of being alone. Of having nightmares that are too real and the one thing you love is the catalyst for the recurring horror of it all."

She turned and ran from the room, down the stairs and along the hallway to her bedroom. She shut and locked the door behind her. What she didn't say was that even Lincoln was a painful reminder of what she could never have, as well.

Lincoln decided it was best to leave Desiree alone. It was apparent that all he'd attempted to do to help only made things worse. He walked into the living room to the bar and fixed himself a glass of rum and Coke.

He took his drink and turned on the stereo, slipping in his Kem CD. As the cool, jazzy sounds of the crooner's voice gently filled the room, Lincoln leaned back against the couch cushions and sipped his drink, contemplating the past few days and especially the events of the evening.

It didn't make sense to him that Desiree didn't want to report what happened in her apartment to the police. Although her explanation sounded somewhat reasonable, he still had big doubts in his mind. If that guy would go so far as to practically rape her, what else was he capable of? He shuddered to think what would have happened had he not shown up when he did. He still had not told her about his conversation with her mother. Everything happened too fast, and now definitely was not a good time.

Lincoln sighed deeply and looked down the hall to where Desiree barricaded herself in her room. He'd heard the lock click on the door. Was she afraid of him, too? Or was it simply another one of her indirect "stay away from me" messages?

He couldn't figure her out. One minute she acted as if things could be the same between them and then the next she acted as if he were her sworn enemy. Whatever it was, he was just as determined to get to the bottom of it all. He was not going to let her walk away from him this time.

Lincoln put his half-finished drink down on the coffee table, picked up the remote, aimed it at the television and put it on mute. At least the TV would keep him company.

He must have dozed off, because the next thing he heard was a piercing scream that raised the hairs on his arms. He jumped up, disoriented and looked around in the semidark room. The scream came again, more intense this time.

Scrambling to his feet, he ran down the hall to Desiree's room.

"Desi!" He pounded on the door. "Desi!"

He heard sobbing coming from the other side. He tried the knob. The door was locked. He rammed his shoulder against it...once, twice. The third time it gave way and the lock broke free from the frame. What he saw when he burst through the door chilled him to his bones.

Chapter 30

Lincoln ran into the room to where Desiree was huddled in a corner, crying hysterically.

"Desi." He got down on the floor next to her and put his arms around her shaking shoulders. "It's okay. I'm here." He looked around the room, thinking the worst.

"Fire…smoke…I can't breathe." She coughed and gagged as if she were back in the burning room.

"Desiree, you're safe. There's no fire." He stroked her face and turned her head to look at him. "There's no fire, Desiree."

Desiree blinked several times until Lincoln came into focus. She snapped her head around and took in her surroundings. She grabbed Lincoln's shirt, then pressed her face against his chest.

"It's okay, baby. Come on, let me help you." He got her to her feet and walked with her over to the bed. "Lie down. Relax. Can I get you anything?"

She shook her head as she stretched out on the bed on her side. He sat next to her. "Try to get some rest." He brushed her damp hair away from her forehead. "I'll be right in the next room if you need me."

"No! Please don't leave me." She sat up. "Please."

"Okay, okay. Relax. I'll stay right here." He settled her back down and pulled the covers up over her shoulders.

"Do you want to talk about it?" he asked gently.

She was silent for a few minutes and then began to speak in slow measured tones. "It was like I was back in the room again and I couldn't get out. I was choking and smoke and fire were everywhere." She shuddered.

Lincoln rubbed her back. "You're safe here with me."

"When is it going to stop, Lincoln? I can't live like this." She pressed her face against his chest and he held her close.

"Time is a great healer," he said. "Give yourself some time."

She sighed heavily, eased back and curled her body into the fetal position on the bed. "I thought that's what I was doing when I came to Sag Harbor."

"Did you have the nightmares there?"

She shook her head. "No." Her eyes found his. "I was almost starting to feel like myself again."

"You should have stayed."

"Maybe," she murmured. "But I'll never really feel better if I don't get to the bottom of what's really bothering me. I have to find some way to get beyond the images and sense of helplessness. The worst part of it is that it's all brought on by the very thing that I love."

"I still think the only way to beat it is to pick up a brush and paint it out of your system—one stroke at a time."

Her stomach knotted.

"And you will when you're ready. There's plenty to keep us busy until then. Tell me a little more about this friend of yours, Allison."

Desiree propped a pillow under her head and began telling him all about Allison's current assignment and her connections to Jackson.

"My suggestion is that we get this Jackson guy involved as soon as possible. I want him on that creep Hampton like white on rice." The night table rattled as his fist connected with it. "He can't get away with what he did to you." He turned to look at her. "Had he ever tried anything like that before?"

"No. The most he's ever done is to ask me out to dinner."

"Did you go?" he asked, a flash of jealousy sparking in his dark eyes.

"Of course not," she snapped. "I had no intention of mixing business with pleasure."

"Well, it's pretty apparent that he can't take no for an answer."

"Let's not talk about Carl anymore tonight," she said, watching the muscles tense beneath the taut brown flesh of Lincoln's face. She instinctively sensed that he was getting himself worked up again.

She patted his arm. "Thank you," she said in a soft whisper.

He raised his head and looked at her. Cautiously he extended his finger and traced her jawline. A delicious shiver ran along Desiree's spine and her eyelids momentarily fluttered.

"Don't you know by now that I would do anything in this world for you? I tried to believe that yes, I once loved you, and that there was still a soft spot in my heart for you and nothing more. When I saw you again I knew it was a lie. I love you as much now as I did then. It hasn't changed. And I'm here for you, Desiree. You don't have to deal with any of this by yourself."

She cupped his face in her hands and rose up on her knees. In the moment that her lips met his, all the loneliness, the fear and the sorrow vanished. The years apart were gone when he pressed a bit harder and wrapped his arms around her and she could feel his heart pound against her breasts.

Tentatively he teased her lip with the tip of his tongue until her mouth slowly opened in welcome.

The sweetness of her mouth worked like an aphrodisiac and raced straight to his head before setting off sparks in his limbs.

Desiree sighed into his mouth while his tongue

teased and explored, reacquainting himself with her taste and textures. Her nimble painter's fingers massaged and caressed his broad back as she visualized those hard muscles and the three-inch scar he'd gotten as a child when he fell out of a tree.

His hands found her waist and his thumbs toyed with the elastic band of her sweatpants, teasing her skin until it began to warm beneath his fingertips. Bold now, he slid his hands under her T-shirt and across her back.

Lincoln's fingers felt like hot coals, Desiree thought, and desperately wanted their heat to ignite the rest of her body.

She eased back, breaking the seal of their kiss. She traced his lips with her fingers and relished in seeing the passion dance in his gaze. The way he looked at her with such hunger raised the peaks of her nipples to hardened pebbles simply by imagining what he could do if he put his mouth…right there.

She lifted her T-shirt over her head and guided his hands to the front clasp of her bra.

Lincoln's breathing rose at the sight of her. Her breasts were still exquisite, round and slightly firm, with perfect nipples that begged to be taken into his mouth. He teased them first with the pads of his thumbs while he massaged and played with the weight of her breasts in his hands.

Her soft sigh and the instinctive movement of her body only heightened Lincoln's desire for her. He took one nipple into his mouth and ran his tongue across it

slow and teasing as if it were a piece of delectable chocolate.

Desiree shuddered—her moan heavy and filled with
longing. But Lincoln took his time. It had been five
years since he'd made love to this woman of his dreams
and he had no intention of running to the finish line
now.

Desiree worked the buttons of his shirt until his bare
chest was exposed. She played with the warm skin, her
fingers skimming from his neck down to the waist of
his pants where she was stopped by the belt and zipper.
But without hesitation she unfastened the belt and made
quick work of the zipper.

Seconds later she held him in her hand and a rush
roared through her body, making her momentarily
light-headed. He was just as she remembered—only
better, if that was possible. The velvet feel of his skin
covering the length and breadth and hardness of him
always drove her wild. She began stroking him, creating a hot pocket with her hands, a mere hint of what
she would feel like inside.

"Desi," he groaned and eased her back onto the
tumble of overstuffed pillows. "I've dreamed about
this," he murmured as he placed kisses along her neck.
"More times than I can count." He kicked out of his
pants and tossed them to the floor. "I want to make you
remember tonight." He took a nipple into his mouth and
suckled it. Her body arched in response. "And what I'm
going to give you every night from now on."

He stretched her out on the bed and slid off her sweatpants and her red thong panties. She still wore red, he thought with a smile.

The perfect dark triangle between her thighs glistened at the tip, beckoning him to sample the nectar that flowed in readiness.

He knelt above her, heating her flesh with his gaze as his eyes trailed the length of her naked form.

"You're still so beautiful," he said barely above a whisper.

She reached up for him, pulling him down to her. With a hunger that frightened her she held him, kissing him with all the desire and longing that had been stamped out by years of neglect. She hadn't been with another man since the day she left Lincoln's apartment five years earlier. It was almost as if she'd saved herself for this very moment.

Lincoln moved her arms from around him and began a slow, mind-blowing tour of her body. His mouth did things to her overheated skin that should have been illegal. He played, he teased, he nibbled, he caressed. He toyed with the tender inside of her thighs until she began to whimper and tremble.

Gently he spread her thighs and his penis pumped and throbbed in response to the pink wet wall that dared him to venture inside.

Lincoln lowered his head and let his tongue flick over the hardened swell of her sex. She cried out and gripped a handful of sheet in her fists as her body arched in response. He delighted in her reaction and worked twice as hard to please her.

Desiree tried to contain the surge of pleasure that rolled through her in waves, but she couldn't as a powerful climax gripped her and wouldn't let go.

Light and dark danced behind her eyes as the electric jolts jerked her entire body, forcing Lincoln to firmly grip her hips and keep them both from being tossed off the bed.

By degrees her cries quieted to sexy purrs and her unbridled thrashing settled into intermittent shudders.

Lincoln caressed her body, every inch of her skin supple and warm to the touch. He kissed her tenderly at the center of her heat before easing up the length of her body until he could look down into her eyes.

"Look at me," he said, his voice raw with need.

Slowly Desiree's eyes fluttered open.

With either hand he lifted her parted thighs and braced them against his forearms and her legs across his back.

"Remember this," he whispered as he pushed deep inside her in one long stroke.

Desiree opened her mouth but no words could escape to describe the exquisite euphoria that filled every crevice of her being.

Tears wells in her eyes as Lincoln began to move in and out of her, stirring up sensations that were even more powerful than his oral exploration of her. Her legs tightened around him and her fingers pressed into his spine when she recognized that in moments both of them would climax together.

Bright white pinpoints of light burst behind Lincoln's lids. He felt as if his entire body gave way, his spirit separating from his body to merge with hers. He felt her contracting and releasing around him, bringing on another release that shook him to his core.

She held him like someone gripping a life raft in the middle of the Atlantic Ocean as wave upon wave of pleasure rolled through her.

Damp, hearts racing, and feeling totally satisfied, they lay tangled in each other's embrace.

Desiree rested her head on Lincoln's chest, soothed by the rhythmic beating of his heart. Her body hummed the way it could only after being loved the way she had been. She listened without comment to Lincoln's words of love and hope for the future for them.

But instead of allowing herself to truly usher in the glow of his love, she silently anguished over what had transpired between them and worried about how she would be able to tell him that it could never happen again.

Chapter 31

The aroma of home fries, eggs and bacon drifted to Desiree, gently stirring her from sleep.

She stretched her arms above her head, causing the sheet to slip down, revealing her nakedness. The previous night with Lincoln raced back to her mind with blinding speed. Her body tingled in response and then her reality slowly settled in.

Turning on her side, she listened to the sounds of pots, running water and Lincoln's deep baritone as he sang along with Luther.

It would be so easy to slip into a relationship with Lincoln again, allow herself to fully love him again. But she knew how unfair that would be to him. She knew how much he wanted a family and she couldn't do that to him. She loved him enough to let him find his happiness with someone who could give him what he wanted.

She looked across the room and found her discarded clothing folded neatly on the chair in the corner. She smiled. Lincoln was always the more organized of the two, a trait that had pleasantly surprised her when they moved in together. He took pride in a neat place and slowly got her into the habit of organizing everything from her clothes and art supplies to her time. It had served her well over the years, especially when she started running her own business.

Lincoln was everything a woman could want: kind, generous, intelligent, a wonderful lover, a savvy businessman and handsome to boot. He'd make some lucky woman a wonderful husband and father to their children.

Her heart ached knowing that the lucky woman could never be her.

She pulled herself out of bed, crossed the room to the dresser and took out a clean set of underwear, then went to the closet and chose a plain white cotton blouse and a pair of jeans.

After a quick shower and getting dressed she entered the kitchen where Lincoln was just putting breakfast on the table.

"Morning," she said.

Lincoln looked up from what he was doing. A slow smile moved across his mouth. "Morning, baby. Breakfast is just about ready. Didn't want to wake you." He came around the table to stand in front of her. He leaned down and kissed her lightly on the mouth. "Did you sleep okay?" He touched her cheek.

"Yes, I did," she said, realizing just how soundly she'd slept and knowing the reason why. She stepped out of his space and moved toward the table. "You?" she asked over her shoulder.

Lincoln frowned for a moment, taken aback by her suddenly cool behavior, a far cry from the woman who lay beneath him the night before.

"Slept fine." He tossed the dish towel he was holding onto the Formica counter and watched her as she seemed to intentionally keep her back to him. "You want to tell me what's going on with you this morning?"

He could always read her, she thought. "Nothing," she murmured and picked up a glass and filled it with orange juice.

Lincoln counted to ten, determined to keep a lid on his bubbling temper. He knew she was still in a fragile state mentally and emotionally, but her maddening habit of evasiveness drove him to the edge.

"Let's eat," he said from between his teeth.

They sat on opposite sides of the table like sparring partners, the only sounds were the clinking of forks against china. Desiree kept her eyes on her food as if it held some vital secret.

Lincoln couldn't stand the silence any longer. "You

want to tell me what's on your mind? And please don't insult me by saying nothing."

Desiree glanced at him for a hot second and looked away. She tried to frame the words she needed to say so that they wouldn't sound so harsh and cold.

"Last night…"

"What about last night? Are you going to tell me what a big mistake it was?"

She put down her fork and looked directly at him for the first time. "Yes."

Lincoln blew out a breath of annoyance and clenched his teeth. "Why did I know that's what you were going to say?" He pushed away from the table with such force that the glasses on the table shook.

He stood and glared down at her. "What is it, Desiree? Why is it so damned hard for you to give anything of yourself except to your work? Is it really about your father or is it just me?"

"What!" Her eyes flashed. "What does my father have to do with anything?"

"I took a trip to see your mother before I came to your apartment."

She leaped up from her seat in a face-off. Her voice lowered. "You did what?" she asked, enunciating every word.

"I didn't stutter. I went to see your mom in the hope that she would be able to give me some insight into what makes you tick." His tone softened, as did his steel expression. "She told me that your father died on your birthday and that it happened right in front of you." He saw her lips tremble as she fought not to cry. "She said you lived for your father and when he died, so did a part of you right along with him."

Desiree tugged in air through her nose and blinked rapidly. The pain and the feeling of immense loss and abandonment were as raw and fresh at that moment as they had been all those many years ago. She adored her daddy, worshipped the ground he walked on and basked in his love and praise of her.

She could still see so clearly her father's big smile and feel his strong arms as he'd lift her into the air and swing her around. Sometimes she could still hear the sound of his voice when he'd read to her at night and tell her that she was his special little girl.

And then one day he was gone, gone into a dark, deep hole, the same hole that had been carved out in her heart. She was crying openly now as the memories of that summer morning ran through her mind…

She'd been getting dressed, preparing for her big birthday party. She was so excited. Her father had arranged for a clown and a pony. All of her neighborhood friends and her friends from school were coming and she couldn't wait for the festivities to start.

"Let me tie your ribbons," her mother had said as she fastened the back buttons on Desiree's party dress.

Desiree turned from the mirror. "Can Daddy do it?" she asked. "Please? I want him to see how pretty I look."

Her mother gave her an indulgent smile. "All right but hurry up. Your guests will be here soon."

Desiree darted out of her bedroom and out into the backyard where her father was putting the finishing touches on the tent.

"Daddy! Daddy!" she called out as she ran across the freshly cut grass, her long ponytails flying behind her.

He turned and a smile of pure delight bloomed across his wide mouth. But just as he started to speak a stricken, panicked look froze his features. He clutched his chest and seemed to gasp for air before he went to the ground like a fallen oak tree.

Desiree stopped running and stood rooted to the spot. A fear like nothing she'd ever felt before gripped her heart and she went completely cold.

"Daddy," she said. "Daddy, get up." Hesitantly and then with urgency she ran to where her father lay face-down in the grass and dirt. She shook his shoulder. "Daddy, Daddy." Her stomach rolled over and over. "Please wake up," she whimpered. He didn't move.

She sat as still as stone, unable to move. Slowly she lowered her head and rested it on his back. She wrapped her arms around him as the skies suddenly opened and the rain came down.

Lincoln held her as she released the years of hurt, the loss and loneliness.

"Your father always wanted the best for you, baby. He wouldn't have wanted you to go through life being afraid of loving. He taught you how to love, and what it was. He couldn't have wanted you never to share what he'd shared with you."

"I've been so afraid, Lincoln. Afraid of losing what I love again." She looked at him, her eyes glistening with tears. "I believed that if I left you before you left me I would be safe." That much was true, she thought, leaving out her doctor's diagnosis of infertility. "So I put all of my emotions into my work and I lost that, too."

"You haven't lost. You've been sideswiped. Obstacles have been set up in front of you. But I know it's in you to go around them—find a way." He took a breath and tried to find the right words that would hit a chord and break through. "Desi, listen, if you were as incapable, as vulnerable as you would like me to believe, there is no way that you could have come as far as you have.

"We all carry scars and wounds from our pasts. It's all part of life. But we have choices. We can either choose to succumb to the injustices or we can choose to win and overcome them. But often we can't do it alone. You've spent your life locked up inside yourself, afraid to reach out for help or support. Every weight is always lighter if we share it." He lifted her chin with the tip of his index finger, compelling her to look at him. "Let me share the weight, Desiree. If you truly give us a chance, there's nothing that we can't overcome together. But you have to want it as much as I do."

"What if I lose you, too? What if you…found out that I couldn't make you happy?"

"How could you ever think that? All I want is you."

He searched her eyes, looking for the answers that were missing in her words.

She moved away from him and crossed the room, putting as much distance as possible between them. She kept her gaze pinned to the floor when she finally spoke.

"I'm not the woman you think I am."

His chuckle was stilted. "What does that mean?"

She swallowed hard and dug deep for the courage to find the words that had haunted her for the past five years.

"After…I…we lost the baby…when I went back to the doctor for my six-week checkup, she told me that there'd been some damage and that the chances were very slim that I could…" She folded her arms and leaned her hip against the counter as much for support as bravado.

"That you could what?" The answer was in her eyes, the way she held on to her body, but she needed to say the words and let them go.

"That I could ever have any more children." She glanced at him for an instant and looked away, afraid of what she might see in his eyes.

A deafening silence filled the kitchen.

"I should have known. Why didn't you tell me, why did you think you had to lie to me and tell me that everything was fine?" he asked gently.

"I didn't want you feeling sorry for me or staying with me because you felt obligated. I wasn't…I'm not a real woman anymore," she tossed out, suddenly defensive.

"If you can still say that, then you haven't understood anything I've been telling you, woman. I love you. Do you understand that? Do you understand what it means? It's not just a word or a feeling, it's a commitment." He cut short the space that separated them until he was close enough to feel the heat rise from her body. "That means through good and bad times, sickness or health, broke or rich. I could never think differently about you."

Her voice cracked when she spoke. "I'm not a real woman anymore."

"Baby." He pulled her into his arms and held her tight. "Don't say that. Don't you dare say that. It takes more than having babies to be a woman."

"That's not what my family thinks, what society thinks. I'll never be able to tell my family."

He stepped back and held her at arm's length. "Is that what's at the heart of it—what your family will think of you?" he asked, not wanting to believe it.

"They all have children. They live to populate the world. Motherhood is a rite of passage for the Armstrong women."

"Your life is not about 'them.' It's about you and how you feel about yourself."

She pulled away. "That's easy for you to say. It's not happening to you. It's not you that relatives will discuss over the dinner table or look at with pity in their eyes at family gatherings. It's me!"

"Desi, since you're so worried about what everyone thinks, do you want to know what I think? Do you care?"

She looked at him defiantly. "No."

"I'm going to tell you anyway. It doesn't matter to me."

"Don't lie to me, Lincoln, just to make me feel better. I know how much you wanted children."

"Not as much as I want you. If we can't have children, that's something I can live with. But I don't want to live out the rest of my life without you in it."

"What if years from now you regret your decision?" she asked in a tentative voice.

"The only thing I would regret is letting you go and allowing you to believe that you're not all the woman I could ever want."

"Do you really mean that?"

"Every word." He waited a moment. "Do you love me, Desiree, really love me?"

Her heart pounded. She knew what he was asking. He was asking for a commitment. Could she honestly give it to him? Could she beat back the demons that plagued her and open herself up to this man without hesitation?

"Yes," she finally said and it was as if a heavy burden had been lifted from her soul.

She felt light, almost giddy. A smile of joyful acceptance brightened her eyes and practically lit up the room.

"Yes, yes, I love you." She ran into his arms, giving in totally to the feel of him, allowing his strength to become hers.

Their kiss was gentle, yet filled with longing and hope for their future.

"I'm always here for you," Lincoln whispered against her pliant mouth. "You'll never be alone again. I promise you."

She wrapped her arms around him. "Make love to me," she said, her words urgent and full of need.

"Nothing would give me more pleasure." He took her hand and led her to his bedroom.

Chapter 32

Cynthia awoke with a throbbing headache. She could barely open her eyes against the high noon sun. She squinted against the light and it only made matters worse.

She groaned as she tried to figure out why she felt so utterly horrible. Slowly, in bits and pieces, like a movie being edited, the previous night began to take shape.

She groaned again when she thought about how many drinks she'd had. Then, how in the world had she gotten home in the condition she knew she must have been in?

Gingerly she stood and walked with great trepidation toward the window. She peered through the slats in the blinds. Parked below was her car.

She didn't remember driving home. She glanced down at herself and saw that she was still fully clothed.

Cynthia pressed her fingers to her temples and gently massaged them, hoping to still the thumping that beat in her head like a rock band.

She was inching past her dresser on the way to the bathroom when she noticed a note propped up against the mirror.

Rest well. I hope you don't feel too bad in the morning and that you'll let me see you again. Lance. His phone number and a cell number were below his name.

Cynthia stared at the note until a faint image of Lance began to take form. Had anything happened between them? She was suddenly worried. But she still had all her clothes on. Hopefully that counted for something. If she had been as inebriated as she thought, why in the world would he want to see her again?

She folded the note and stuck it in the top drawer of the dresser. Maybe after a shower and a steaming cup of black coffee her head would clear. She crept to the bathroom, careful not to rattle her head with heavy footsteps.

Dressed in a worn jogging outfit and fluffy slippers, Cynthia sipped her coffee. Yesterday had been one for the record books, she thought. It was the confrontation with her mother that had sent her to a bar—alone—to wash away her sorry mother-daughter relationship.

Why couldn't her mother simply love and respect her

for who she was instead of working so hard to make her and her life appear so worthless and insignificant?

All her life she'd desperately wanted a relationship with her mother, but it was not to be.

But there was something else bothering her, something nagging in the back of her head that had nothing to do with the receding headache, but she couldn't quite grasp it. Whatever it was had to do with her visit to her mother's house.

Frowning in thought, she tried to figure it out, but the answer eluded her. Maybe it would come to her later, she concluded, and tried to push the unsettling feeling aside.

Cynthia checked the time on the clock that hung above the refrigerator. It was already three o'clock. More than half the day was gone and it had been uneventful, frustrating and lonely. What she craved was company, someone to talk to.

Pushing back from the table, she returned to her bedroom and retrieved the note from Lance. She sucked on her bottom lip debating whether or not to call. She couldn't make any more of a fool of herself than she'd already done, she thought, taking the note and walking to the phone on the nightstand.

She sat down on the side of the bed and picked up the phone. "Here goes nothing," she murmured.

"Tell me about this investigator, Jackson," Lincoln said as he spooned with Desiree and kissed the back of her neck.

"It's kind of hard to concentrate with you doing that," she said, her voice thick and soft.

"Hmm. I can give you something hard if that's what you really want," Lincoln said in a voice filled with need.

"Behave," she warned without bite.

"Can't a guy have any fun?"

She turned over onto her other side to face him. "You've had enough fun to last you at least until to-night."

"That's what you say. I'm a growing boy," he taunted, reaching for her hand to wrap around his sex.

"Oooh, so I see." Her lids grew heavy as she stroked him to climax and listened to his moans of pleasure. She smiled, relishing in her power to arouse him, to satisfy him.

They lay curled in each other's arms.

"I owe you one," he said, catching his breath.

"I'm sure you'll find a way to repay me." She kissed his lips.

They were quiet for a while, basking in the afterglow of rediscovering each other.

This was the way it had been between them in the early years of their relationship, Desiree thought. They couldn't wait to get at each other with a hunger that seemed insatiable at times. There had been other men in her life before Lincoln, but none who could compare to him as a lover, none who could take her to the heights she reached with him.

Yes, she'd missed him, missed him more than she had ever been willing to admit, even to herself. The years that she had locked herself away from Lincoln and the possibility of love had changed her, made her distant and cautious with men. She didn't want to risk her heart, or better, her body, with someone else. There were times when she'd been tempted to cross that line, but there was a part of her that inexplicably felt that she would be betraying Lincoln—even though they were apart. Silly, she mused, but it was how she'd felt. She was the reason that their relationship had been severed. She was the one who walked away from all that he offered. She'd been so afraid that he would somehow think less of her, love her less, that she would see the pity in his eyes, his loss of a family. And that was what she could not bear.

That was all behind them now. She should have trusted his love. Now she did. She would take him at his word that what he wanted was her, no matter what. With that thought to sustain her, she could deal with anything, even losing her own dream.

She kissed his cheek and his eyes fluttered open. A slow smile spread across his mouth as if seeing her was the most wonderful thing in the world to him.

"I was having the best dream," he said in a still sleepy voice.

"What were you dreaming?" She traced his brows with her fingertip.

"Hmm, we were on a sailboat, out by The Port. The

day was absolutely perfect. You had on the cutest short set," he said, and playfully pinched her bare buttocks. "It left little to the imagination."

"And what did *you* have on?"

"A pair of cutoff jeans and nothing else." He smiled wickedly.

"Then what happened?"

"We sailed and talked, really talked, about our lives, what we wanted for ourselves and our future." He looked into her eyes. "We can make it, Desi. I know we can."

"So do I," she readily admitted. "I know that now. I've been such a fool to have wasted so much time, time we can never get back."

"None of that matters anymore, baby. The only thing that matters is now, and what we do from here on out."

She nodded her head in agreement. "First thing tomorrow, I want to stop by Rachel's house and pick up the paints and canvases that you bought for me."

Lincoln propped himself up on his elbow. "Are you sure?"

"Definitely. It's time. If there is one thing I've discovered in just the short time we've been back together, it's that I can't continue to live in fear or live in the past. What happened at the gallery was horrible and I'll feel the loss for a long time. But I can't let it cripple me and stop me from what I love to do. And I have you to thank for that. For pushing possibility in my face and making me look at it, daring me to dream again."

"All I want, all I've ever wanted was your happiness, in whatever form that took. But I know you. And I know that art runs in your veins. It nourishes you like the average person gets nourishment from food and water. No matter what I did or didn't do, I know that at some point you would have been able to cross that line yourself. You're too tough to let life beat you down. It was all temporary."

She grinned. "Yeah, I am kinda tough—sometimes."

"No one on this planet can be more determined or single-minded than you. You've had your share of trauma and you weathered the storm."

"What storms have you weathered?"

He shrugged slightly. "I guess my biggest hurdle was growing up in foster care after my folks passed, moving from one family to the other, never knowing when the social worker was going to come and take me to the next stop." He laughed without humor. Desiree stroked his arm.

"I can't imagine what that must have been like for you. Coming from a big family...I know that's why family and roots are so important to you."

He tugged in a long breath and let it go. "I suppose so."

She cupped his face and forced him to look at her. "That's why I want you to be absolutely sure that staying with me and us not being able to have kids is what you really want, Lincoln. I don't want you to regret it."

"You're all I want," he said, with all the sincerity in

his soul. "I'm very sure." He pulled her close. "Now that we have that settled—because it is settled—tell me about this investigator."

"Well, as I mentioned, I ran into Allison, an old college friend from Howard University…"

Lincoln listened, putting the pieces together in his head.

"So your friend is working on an investigative piece on insurance fraud schemes."

"Right. And when I started talking about my situation she mentioned Jackson, the husband of another college friend, Carly." Desiree sat up in bed. "As a matter of fact I was supposed to talk to Allison today."

She tossed off the sheet and made a slow, teasing game of stretching her nakedness across Lincoln's body to get the phone from the nightstand. And he took every available advantage that was boldly laid out in front of him for the taking.

He lifted her on top of him and nibbled her neck, then eased down until a delectable nipple teased his lips.

Desiree released a soft moan as she pressed her pelvis against his and dialed the number that she'd committed to memory. It took all of her concentration to keep her mind on the prompts of Allison's answering machine and leave a message that made sense. She pressed the appropriate buttons and Lincoln pressed all of hers. She could barely get the words out when Lincoln pushed up inside her, making her gasp into the phone. He moved in a steady circular motion until Desiree felt as if she were on fire.

The phone fell to the floor and there was no telling what Allison would hear when she got the message.

Desiree braced her weight on her calves and forearms and took her time showing him that she could give just as good as she got.

"At some point we should get up and eat," Lincoln said as he stretched his long limbs like a lazy panther and stood.

"I am starved. I'll flip you for who cooks."

He turned to her. "As a tribute to our reuniting, let's go out and eat."

"I knew there was a reason why I liked you," she said with a grin.

"You wound me. I thought it was my sexy smile."

"Not!" She got up, grabbed one of Lincoln's shirts out of the closet and put it on. "As long as it's no place fancy," she said, heading for the shower. "Just someplace cozy and with good food."

"Sounds fine to me. Don't be too long," he called out as she shut the door. "I remember growing gray hair waiting for you to come out of the shower."

Desiree pulled open the bathroom door and threw a towel with dead aim that beaned him right on the head. She quickly closed and locked the door before he had a chance to retaliate.

Lincoln laughed out loud, picked up the towel from the floor and spotted the discarded phone. He picked it up, disconnected the line, then listened for the telltale beeps to indicate waiting messages. When he heard the tones he dialed his code. There were two messages, both of them from Allison.

The first one was apparent that she was having fun at their personal expense, reenacting the sounds of their lovemaking. She closed her blow-by-blow commentary with "I hope I have as much fun as you two seem to be having when my husband gets home. You go, girl! I guess I should call back."

The second message wasn't as fun-filled.

Chapter 33

Cynthia was still stunned at her out-of-character move of calling Lance. Getting men was something she'd never really had a problem with; the problem was keeping them. For some reason she seemed to scare men off. She wasn't sure if they simply had no interest in her, or if somehow her mother had gotten to them and scared them away—or worse, paid them off.

In any event, her once long dance card had dwindled. Her only real friend was Desiree. She enjoyed her company and her offhanded take on life. Desiree was down-to-earth and rarely pulled punches even when she was being polite about telling someone off. Which was one of the things that was driving Desiree to distraction—she couldn't really tell Carl off the way she wanted to.

Cynthia couldn't count the number of times that Desiree had stormed through the store cussing up a storm after one of Carl's impromptu visits. He truly rubbed her the wrong way and he was totally clueless. But if he did know, he didn't care. It was plain to anyone watching that Carl Hampton had the hots for Desiree Armstrong.

Cynthia peered closer in the mirror and applied her mascara. Carl Hampton was the kind of man her mother would love to see her with. She cringed. He might be wealthy and actually handsome, but there was just something about him that she didn't like.

She stepped back and assessed her handiwork. Satisfied that she'd added just enough of everything, she went in search of her cream-colored sling backs. They would go perfectly with the spaghetti-strapped sheath she selected in a cool melon color. She wanted to look soft and feminine but not obvious. However, anything would be an improvement over how she must have looked last night. She stepped into her shoes just as the doorbell rang.

"Right on time. I like that."

But as she walked toward the door her confidence began to wane. Had she been so desperately lonely that she was willing to call up a virtual stranger and take him up on his offer?

The bell rang again. Perhaps she should cut her losses and pretend she wasn't home. She bit down on her thumbnail, a nervous childhood habit. Well, she thought, putting one foot in front of the other, desperate times called for desperate measures. She tugged in a breath, put on her best smile and opened the door.

When she did, her stomach did a funny little dance. Lance was nothing like the fuzzy image that she remembered. He was moderately tall, about an even six feet, with sable-brown hair parted on the side and the darkest blue eyes she'd ever seen.

"Remember me?" he asked, with a gentle smile.

"Yes, but trust me, this is much better." She laughed self-consciously. "Come in." She stepped aside and let him pass, catching a quick whiff of his cologne, which reminded her of pure clean. Nice, she thought. "Can I get you anything."

"No, I'm fine," he said, turning to her and sliding his hands into his pants pockets. "I didn't really get a chance to look around last night. You have a very nice place."

"Thank you. And thank you for bringing me home… safely."

"Don't mention it. I see you read a lot." He walked toward the wall-to-wall bookcase in the open living room. "Mostly art books, I see."

"Something I thought I wanted to be when I grew up." She followed him into the living room.

He angled his head toward her in question. "Something you wanted to be?"

"I have a great love for art. I just don't have the skills needed to be a real artist."

"Hmm. It's all very subjective, you know. One man's trash is the next man's Picasso."

They laughed.

"True," Cynthia said. "Have a seat, if we're not in a hurry."

"Thanks. I figured we'd play it by ear." He sat at the end of the eggshell-colored couch. "I wasn't really sure what you liked to eat and I didn't want to assume."

"That's refreshing."

"What is?"

"The idea that you didn't want to assume you knew my tastes and were actually willing to wait and ask. Most men don't do that."

"Maybe you've been hanging out with the wrong crowd."

"I'm beginning to think so." She sat opposite him on the matching love seat. "So what do you do? I'm sure you told me, but I couldn't tell you." She crossed her long legs.

For a moment Lance's gaze traveled up and down the length of her shapely calf, then focused on her face. "I'm a playwright."

Her eyes widened. "A playwright. Wow. I've never met a playwright before."

He chuckled at her reaction. "We're a pretty ordinary bunch."

She leaned forward. "What have you written?"

He ran off a short list of plays and she was even more

surprised to discover that she'd heard of some and had seen others.

"I really am impressed."

"Thanks."

Now his name was ringing the right bells. Lance Freeman, the playwright, sitting in her living room. She frowned.

"I could have sworn you told me you were a shrink." She looked at him askance.

"What I said was I listened to people for a living and you asked if that made me a shrink. I said some might say that. I do listen to people for a living. That's how I come up with ideas for my plays and develop characters, by listening." He stretched his arm out across the back of the couch.

"I'm not going to wind up the drunk blonde in your next play, am I?"

He chuckled. "I would never be that obvious. So... tell me about this art thing that you *don't* do."

Cynthia explained what had been her position at the gallery and all that had transpired.

"Wow. I remember reading about that in the paper. So what do you plan to do now?"

"I'm not sure really. A lot depends on Desiree. I'd love to continue working for her."

"Ever think about opening your own gallery?"

"Hmm, not really. Why?"

"Maybe you should." He stood up. "We should get

going. If we get an early dinner, perhaps we can catch a movie if you're up for it."

"Sounds perfect."

Desiree finally emerged from the bathroom.

"All yours," she announced, crossing the room wrapped in a towel.

"Allison called while we were… She said she has some information for you and wants you to call her." Lincoln handed Desiree the sheet of paper with Allison's phone number on it. "She said she wasn't at home but left this number and said it was important that you reach her."

Desiree took the paper from him and sat down next to him on the bed. She reached for the phone. "Did she say what it was?"

"No, just that you should call as soon as you could. She, uh…heard us."

Desiree made a face. "Oooh. Maybe I'll tell her it was a movie." She laughed and punched in the number. The phone rang three times before Allison picked up.

Desiree spoke with her for a few minutes, then looked at Lincoln. "Sure, we can meet you. Just tell me where."

Chapter 34

"What do you think Allison found out?" Desiree asked, suddenly feeling like the lead character in a made-for-television mystery movie. She locked her seat belt and turned to Lincoln with inquiring eyes.

"Got me. But I would guess something important if she wanted to meet with us. If she's working this insurance thing, maybe she's turned up some solid information on Hampton."

"Hmm. I find it hard to believe that Carl would sabotage his own place for money. But stranger things have happened."

"In the years that I've been working construction I've seen all kinds of scams. When people get desperate enough they are liable to do anything."

Desiree thought back to that night in Rachel's apartment when Carl attacked her. "Yes," she said thoughtfully and wrapped her arms around her body.

Lincoln snatched a look in her direction and immediately read her pensive expression. "Do you regret not having called the police?"

"No. I think I did the right thing. I'm sure Rachel wouldn't agree and I know that you don't. Had I been hurt or worse, then yes, I'd want to bury the SOB, but I wasn't. The Man upstairs works in mysterious ways. Whatever is due Carl Hampton he is going to get. I'm not worried about that. What he did was an act of desperation and frustration. As much as he may have come on to me in the past he was never violent."

"Well, I'm down with the retribution part," he said, still seething about what took place. He drove the car around a double-parked van and continued on down the twilit street.

"This really is a beautiful city," Desiree mused as she looked at the stores, spiraling buildings and bright lights.

"There's no place like the Apple. I've been all over and this is the only city where you can walk out of your house in the middle of the night and find a store open."

Desiree chuckled. "I know. You really have a great place, too."

"Thanks. I don't stay there very often. For all the amenities of the city life, I've grown accustomed to staying out by the shore."

"Even in the winter?"

"It's quite beautiful in the winter—peaceful." He turned to her. "You'll see."

Her gaze held his a moment. "I'm looking forward to it."

"When everything settles down we need to make plans."

"Plans? What kind of plans?"

"Plans about us. What we are going to do, where we are going to live."

Desiree's stomach flipped, then settled. "All right," she said quietly.

"Do you have any preferences about where you want to live?"

She glanced out of the window. *Living together again.* The idea excited and frightened her. "I'd like to stay near Manhattan, I think."

"Well, we'll talk about it. I'm open." He peered out the window at the addresses on the block. "There it is." He looked up and down the street for a parking space and circled the block three times before one opened up. "The downside of living in Manhattan," he grumbled, taking the key out of the ignition.

He came around the front and helped Desiree out of the car, then he set the alarm and they walked to the front door of Allison's brownstone.

While they waited for the front door to be answered, Desiree whispered, "I hope she doesn't mention anything about what she heard on the phone."

"I have a funny feeling she will. She sounded like she got a real kick out of it."

"Jeez, it must have sounded like one of those 900 calls."

Lincoln chuckled.

The door was pulled open and Allison appeared looking just as casually chic as she did when Desiree saw her on the train.

"Desi." She leaned forward and hugged her, then turned to Lincoln with a mischievous smile on her face. "And I feel as if I already know you, Lincoln."

"Nice to meet you in person," he playfully retorted.

"Come in. My husband is out of town on business. I wish he could have been here to meet you both." She led them into a sunken living room that was the size of a small basketball court.

"Beautiful place," Desiree said.

"Thanks. We searched for almost a year to find it and then got it for a steal. An old couple had it for decades, no children or greedy relatives, and they wanted to move to Florida. They practically gave it to us."

"I could easily get used to this," Desiree said, taking a seat on the mint-green sectional.

"Can I get either of you something to drink? I fixed something light to eat. So we can munch if you get hungry." Allison sat down and crossed her long, pant-covered legs. She took in both of them with her penetrating gaze. "I know I sounded like a superspy or something on the phone, but believe me, when you've been in the journalism business as long as I have you learn to watch your back. I don't trust saying too much of anything of importance on the phone, especially when I'm working on this kind of story."

"I understand," Lincoln said. "What were you able to find out?"

Allison leaned back. "Well, first of all, Mr. Hampton has skipped town. From what I could find out he's at his place in the Bahamas. That to me spells guilty. Why run if you have nothing to hide?"

"Interesting," Desiree murmured. "He'd mentioned to me several times that he had a place in Nassau. Anything else?"

Allison reached for her notebook on the end table and flipped through a few pages. "Mostly background stuff. I'm checking into his finances now, trying to see if he's in any kind of trouble. That's usually a telltale sign. And from what I can gather from the fire marshal they definitely have ruled it arson." She looked directly at Desiree. "I'm sorry."

Desiree nodded. "Could Carl have been that desperate that he would have set fire to the place and possibly killed me in the process?"

"Anything is possible, Desiree, that's why I called Jackson. He's good at what he does. Folks are only going to tell a reporter so much. He has a way of getting information. I can work my sources and he can work his. I invited him over." She checked her watch. "He should be here shortly. That was the main reason I wanted you to come, so you could meet with him face-to-face."

"Fine. I'll help in any way that I can."

Allison stood. "Excuse me for just one minute." She walked into the kitchen.

Lincoln turned to Desiree. "This sounds like it's really turning into something, something bigger than I thought." He reached for her hand and held it. "It will all work out and whoever is responsible will be dealt with."

"I know." She smiled. "I feel better just knowing that you are around."

"Always." He lightly kissed her lips just as Allison returned with a tray of finger foods: buffalo wings, celery sticks, dip, an assortment of cheeses and crackers.

"Help yourselves," she said, setting the tray down on the coffee table. "What would you like to drink, wine, water, soda, juice?"

"A glass of wine for me," Desiree said.

"Make that two."

Desiree stood. "I'll help you."

They stood next to each other at the wet bar on the far side of the living room.

"He's a cutie-pie," Allison whispered as she took a bottle of chilled white wine from the minirefrigerator.

Desiree giggled. "I know. And thanks."

"I take it things are serious between you two. All

you have to do is look in his eyes and you can see the man is crazy in love with you."

Desiree felt her face heat. "I'm in love with him, too," she readily admitted, and saying it out loud felt good.

Allison poured three glasses of wine and put them on another tray. "I wish you all the happiness in the world," she said. "There's nothing like coming home to someone you love, and you know they love you back."

"I'm looking forward to it."

Just as they set down the glasses the doorbell rang.

"That's Jackson," Allison said and went to the door.

Moments later Jackson Trent walked into the room, and his presence definitely commanded attention. He was well put together in a navy suit that fit the long lines of his well-honed body. He didn't look the part of a scruffy private investigator, but rather a Wall Street banker.

"Jackson, this is Desiree Armstrong and Lincoln Davenport."

Jackson shook Desiree's hand and then Lincoln's. "Good to meet you both." He unbuttoned his jacket and sat down. "Where's Jacob?" he asked Allison.

"Out of town on a book tour. He'll be back on the weekend."

"Good, he owes me on that Knicks game."

Allison laughed and turned to Lincoln and Desiree. "Those two are the ones who should be investigated," she said. "They have more bets going than OTB."

"All in good fun," Jackson said. "Now, I guess you want to know what I found out."

Lincoln and Desiree leaned forward attentively.

"My preliminary information is still a bit sketchy, but my hunch is that Carl didn't have anything to do with the fire."

Desiree's brows rose. "Really?"

"Too simple and too stupid. And from what I've discovered about Carl Hampton, he's anything but stupid. His business on the surface appears solid, but I'm going to check further. I'll be visiting his offices tomorrow." He focused in on Desiree. "Who else works at the gallery?"

"It was just me and my assistant, Cynthia."

"Did the two of you get along?"

"Yes! You don't think Cynthia—"

"I don't put anything past anyone," he said simply. "Did the two of you have any differences, arguments?"

"No, not at all."

"I'll still need her contact information. I'll want to talk to her myself." He pulled a notepad out of his jacket pocket and jotted down the information that Desiree provided. "Is there anyone you can think of that would want to harm you? Any suspicious people lurking around anytime before the fire?"

Desiree was thoughtful for a moment. "No. Not really." She frowned. "There was this woman, though. I didn't think much of it at the time." She turned to Lincoln. "Remember when we were in town at Sag Harbor and I said I ran into someone I thought I knew from the shop but she insisted that we'd never met?"

Lincoln thought back and pointed his finger. "Yes, I remember."

"Could that mean anything?" she asked Jackson.

"At this stage every bit of information is helpful. Do you remember her name?"

"McKay. That's all I remember."

"What did she buy?"

"A small sculpture. She said it was for her daughter."

Jackson nodded and wrote down the information. "Did she have it mailed?"

Desiree's expression dropped. "No. I wrapped it and she took it with her. She paid cash," she added, anticipating his next question.

"Hmm," Jackson murmured. "Tell me some more about Cynthia. Did she have any problems that you were aware of?"

"Nothing specific. I mean just the usual stuff. She always talked about her and her mother's lousy relationship but that was about it."

"Who is her mother?"

"Eleanor Hastings."

Jackson's brows rose. "*The* Eleanor Hastings?"

"Yes."

Jackson nodded. "Maybe I'll pay Ms. Hastings a visit."

"You don't think her mother had anything to do with it?" Allison asked.

"Eleanor Hastings has been notorious in the business world for wheeling and dealing all her life. What she wants she gets. There were rumors that her husband didn't really die of natural causes, but nothing was ever proven."

"Cynthia did mention once that her mother had ruined her life but she was never really specific. I always got the impression that it had to do with a past lover or something."

"I wouldn't put it past Eleanor. If she wants someone out of the way, consider yourself gone."

A chill scurried up Desiree's spine.

"I'm going to look into the old case of her husband and I definitely want to talk to the daughter. She may know something. And if there is anything you can remember about the McKay woman, give me a call." He reached into his pocket and handed Desiree a business card.

"Like I said, I don't believe Carl is behind this. But Eleanor Hastings very well may be."

"But why?" Desiree asked.

"That's what I'm going to try to find out."

Chapter 35

"So tell me about yourself," Lance said as he cut into his steak.

"What would you like to know?"

"Where you grew up, what you like to do, where you went to school." He looked at her and gave an encouraging smile. "Trust me, it won't turn into a stage play."

Cynthia laughed. "Well, I grew up in Manhattan mostly, although we did travel a great deal. My mother," she said the word with disdain, "wanted to be sure that I was well rounded."

"What is it with you and your mother, really? You hinted at it the other night…but you can imagine it all didn't make a lot of sense."

She blushed. "Let's just say that my mother and I

are at odds about any- and everything that has to do with me. She doesn't feel that I live up to the Hastings name."

"Why?"

"She has her vision of who I should be and what my life should be like. And I unfortunately don't fit that image."

"I'm sorry." He picked up his glass in a toast. "If it's any consolation I think you make a great vision."

"Thank you." She lowered her gaze, then looked at him. "You mentioned earlier about me opening my own gallery."

"Yes."

"Do you really think I could?"

"Why not? As you said, you know what you like."

"I know, but it would almost be like doing what my mother wanted. She hates the fact that I work for someone else as a 'lowly assistant,' as she puts it."

"What do you want, Cynthia?"

"I want to be free of her and free to do what I want without recriminations. I want to be happy."

"The key to being happy is discovering it for yourself. You can't live on the whims of others, you'll make yourself crazy. And if I'm not being too bold I think that there is a part of you that wants to please her and you may never be able to do that. The only way around it is to please yourself."

She sipped on her wine. "I know that," she said with a sigh, then brightened. "I do like the idea of opening my own gallery though, something small and intimate. Not too overpriced but with quality stuff."

"If it's what you want, then go for it. The only thing stopping you is yourself."

She was thoughtful for a moment. "I would hate to think that with Desiree's place gone and all her work, people would begin to wonder about me if I opened my own place."

"What do you mean?"

"That maybe I was jealous or something and perhaps had something to do with the fire."

"I wouldn't worry about that. Wouldn't it be a lot easier to simply quit and strike out on your own than to burn a place to the ground?"

She gave him a crooked smile. "I guess you're right."

"You have to stop worrying about what other people think. Live for Cynthia. And if you plan to keep me around, I'm going to continue to remind you of that."

She set down her glass. "What made you want to be bothered with me...especially under the circumstances that we met?"

"Like I said, I study people for a living. I saw something beyond the caustic words and unhappy expression to what you were underneath."

"And what was that?"

"Someone who was searching for something and hadn't quite figured out how to find it."

"Hmmph. That's pretty accurate. Hopefully that will change."

"It will. You have to decide what you want and how

you are going to go about getting it. And you are going to have to accept your relationship with your mother for what it is."

She lowered her head. "I know. Silly girlish dream."

"I wrote a play about that once but never had it produced."

"What, silly girlish dreams?" She chuckled derisively.

"Not really. It was a play about a domineering mother and her daughter and the lengths the mother went through to keep her daughter under her control."

"Sounds like my life."

"Life imitating art." He paused. "I want to ask you something and you don't have to answer if you don't want to."

"Okay."

"You said your mother didn't want you working for someone else."

"Right."

"Do you think that she would do whatever she could to change that?"

"What are you getting at?"

He shook his head. "Never mind. That's the playwright in me talking." He lifted his chin. "Let's eat and talk about something more pleasant."

Cynthia watched him enjoy his meal, and wondered how right he could be.

"Thanks for a great evening. I had a wonderful time," Cynthia said, turning to him at her front door.

"So did I. I hope we can do it again soon."

"We will. Do you want to come in for a few minutes?"

The corner of his mouth lifted in a grin. "I don't think that would be wise, Ms. Hastings. I might lose all my gentlemanly charm."

Her face flushed. "Maybe next time, then."

"I certainly hope so." He leaned forward and kissed her lightly on the cheek. "Good night." He turned and walked away.

Cynthia closed the door, feeling good inside and about herself for the first time in a long while. Other than Desiree, she really had no one who believed in her. Maybe she *could* open her own shop and maybe she would go back to art school and try again. It wasn't as if she didn't have the financial resources to make it happen. The idea was beginning to sound better and better. Maybe she would talk with Desiree about it.

She walked into her bedroom, put her purse down on the nightstand and noticed the flashing light on her answering machine. She depressed the button and listened to the messages. Two were from a catalogue company advising her that her shipment of imported linens were on the way and the last was from Desiree.

"Hi, Cynthia. I want to apologize for disappearing the way I did. I needed to clear my head. But I'm back in the city. I'm staying with a friend. There's someone I've been in touch with who is looking into the fire. His name is Jackson Trent and he wants to talk to you." She left his number. "Please give him a call. It's important. Thanks."

Who was Jackson Trent and why did he want to talk to her?

Chapter 36

Eleanor paced the confines of her bedroom, glaring at the headlines on the third page of the *New York Post*. NEAR FATAL FIRE DECLARED ARSON. She read the article with great interest. "Fool," she said between her teeth. She dismissively tossed the paper on the bed and walked out into the front room.

"Mary! Mary," she called out.

Mary came almost instantly. "Yes, Mrs. Hastings."

"Where's my coffee?"

"It's still brewing," she said.

"At this hour? You've been with me long enough to know that I want my coffee ready when I get up in the morning."

"Sorry, Mrs. Hastings. I wasn't feeling very well this morning. I'm having a slow start."

Eleanor looked her up and down. "Well, you look fine now," she said, her tone not quite as strident.

"I'll bring the coffee right away, ma'am." Mary turned and headed back to the kitchen, her look of barely contained fury shielded from Eleanor.

Mary had been in the employ of the Hastings for more than twenty years. The pay was great. She was able to send her two children to college with the money she made waiting on Eleanor hand and foot. But each day was becoming more difficult. If it were humanly possible, Eleanor Hastings, she'd swear, was becoming more miserable and unbearable each day.

Every morning she had to pray for the strength not to pick up one of her expensive sculptures, hit her over the head, and never lose a night's sleep. And her poor daughter, the way she treated Cynthia was a sin. Mary's heart ached for her. No daughter should have to put up with the abuse that Eleanor meted out to that girl.

Mary poured the coffee into a carafe, cut up two oranges and set them on a plate. She put two pieces of toast in the toaster and put a bowl of jelly on the serving tray.

She would give anything to see Eleanor get what she deserved. No one should go through life treating people the way she did and get away with it.

"Lord, forgive me," she whispered.

"I've given you all I intend to give you," Eleanor was saying into the phone. A scowl crossed her perfectly made-up face. "That's your problem. I would suggest that you take a trip, a long trip. There's nothing to connect us and I will deny ever having known you." She smiled. "And who do you think they will believe?" She hung up the phone, just as Mary came into the room.

"Your breakfast is in the dining room, ma'am."

Eleanor didn't even give Mary the courtesy of an acknowledgment. She simply walked past her as if she were invisible.

Mary glared at her benefactor's back and an old saying from her grandmother came to mind. "God don't like ugly."

"You really need to come back, Carl," Jake Foxx was saying. "People are asking questions that I can't and don't want to answer. It looks really bad with you not being here. And the newspaper article today didn't help the situation." He told him about the story in the *Post*.

Carl cursed beneath his breath.

"And there's some guy named Jackson Trent who was here this morning asking questions."

"Who is he?"

"Some private investigator."

"What?" Carl frowned as he paced the floor of his Nassau bungalow.

Beyond the picture glass window was nothing but white sandy beaches and tranquil blue water. This was his refuge, where he came to be alone, to think and relax. But this visit had been anything but relaxing. He hadn't come simply to rejuvenate, he'd run, like a coward he'd run. It wasn't in his nature to run from trouble. But the truth was, his conscience was killing him. He'd had nightmares about what almost happened with him and Desiree.

"Carl, are you there?" Jake boomed into the phone.

"Yes, I'm here," he said absently.

"Well, what are you going to do?"

"I'll look into the flights and I'll be on the next plane back to New York. I'll call you."

"Things aren't looking good, Carl. Investigators are crawling all over the place, and if another reporter calls… I'm not going to deal with the fallout alone."

"You won't. I'll take care of everything."

He hung up the phone and dialed the airport. It was time he went back and faced the music.

Chapter 37

Cynthia brushed her long hair in front of her dressing table mirror as she waited for Jackson Trent's arrival. She couldn't imagine what she could possibly tell him that she hadn't told everyone else who'd asked.

She'd thought about calling Lance and asking him to come over for moral support, but thought better of it. She was a big girl. She could handle it.

Cynthia checked her watch. When she'd spoken with him earlier that morning, he'd indicated that he'd arrive by three. He still had fifteen minutes.

She studied her reflection in the mirror and was satisfied with the simple outfit she'd chosen. She'd picked out a pale blue silk shirt, a pair of navy pleated slacks and navy loafers. Classy but understated, she thought, taking a final look. She added a thin-as-hair gold chain around her neck just as the bell rang.

Cynthia brushed the front of her blouse and straightened the belt on her slacks. When she went to the door she was surprised and somewhat relieved to find not only Jackson Trent but Desiree and a very handsome escort.

"Desi! My goodness." She held out her arms and embraced Desiree in a tight, long-overdue hug. "You look…happy." Cynthia beamed.

Desiree snatched a look at Lincoln. "I am. Lincoln Davenport, Cynthia Hastings. And this is Jackson Trent."

"Come in, come in." She stepped aside and the trio filed past. "We can sit in the living room." She led them into the finely appointed space. "Make yourselves comfortable. Can I get anyone anything?"

"Some water for me would be fine," Jackson said, taking in the obviously expensive décor. The lady had taste and money, both he was sure she'd inherited from her parents. He wondered if she'd also inherited her mother's ruthlessness disguised behind a facade of good manners and beauty.

"What about you, Lincoln?"

"Nothing for me."

"Desi?"

"You know I love my Diet Pepsi."

Cynthia grinned. "Coming right up."

While Cynthia was pulling out a bottle of Evian from the fridge, Desiree walked up behind her.

"How have you been, Cynthia?"

Cynthia jumped in surprise. She pressed her hand to her chest and turned.

"You need to walk with a heavier footstep." She laughed. "I'm doing fine. But that's what I need to ask you. I've been worried." She handed Desiree a can of Diet Pepsi.

"I've been...slowly getting it together." She bobbed her head. "One day at a time, you know."

Cynthia pulled out a chair from beneath the kitchen table. "Sit. Talk to me for a minute before the inquisition."

"It won't be that bad. Jackson seems pretty cool. Strictly business but decent." She took a seat.

"You want a glass for that?" Cynthia asked, pointing to the can.

"No, I'll take it straight." She chuckled.

"First and foremost, tell me about Mr. Tall, Dark and Handsome," Cynthia said, sitting down opposite Desiree.

Desiree grinned like a kid at Christmas. "I guess I never really told you about Lincoln. We'd just broken up when you and I met. Actually, we were engaged."

"What? Get out of here. And he let you go?"

"It wasn't him. It was me and it's a long story. Anyway, the bottom line is he wound up being the owner of the bed-and-breakfast that I went to stay at in Sag Harbor."

"You're kidding."

"Nope. Talk about fate stepping in and throwing a curve."

"Everything happens for a reason." A secretive smile crept across her mouth. "I met someone, too."

"You did! You'll have to tell me all about him." She squeezed Cynthia's hand.

"I will, but we better get inside before they start watching football or something." She stood.

Desiree laughed. "You're right."

"Not to pry or anything, but where are you staying?"

"For the moment, at Lincoln's place here in the city. I was at Rachel's… I'll tell you all about that, too." She started for the living room.

Cynthia took the bottle of water and filled a glass with ice. "Seems like we have a lot of catching up to do," she said, following Desiree back inside.

"Exactly," Desiree said over her shoulder.

Both men stood when the ladies returned to the room. Once everyone was settled, Jackson got straight to the point.

"Desiree has filled me in on a great deal already," he began. "But I'd still like to hear from you."

"I'm not certain how much more I can add, but I'm happy to help."

"You'd be surprised that what usually turns a case

around is that one bit of information that someone didn't think was important."

Cynthia tugged in a breath and wrapped her hands around her knees. "Ready when you are."

More than an hour later, Jackson completed his interview with Cynthia. He flipped through his notepad, then looked across at her. "Thank you. You've been very helpful." He stood and extended his hand which Cynthia shook. "I'll be in touch if I have any other questions." He handed her a business card. "If you think of anything else, even if it seems unimportant, give me a call."

Cynthia glanced at the card, then tucked it in her pants pocket. "I will."

Lincoln stood up and took Desiree's hand, helping her to her feet. "Good to finally meet you, Cynthia. Desi has only great things to say about you."

"Good to meet you, too, Lincoln. Maybe we could all get together for dinner sometime soon. I'll call you and Desi, and we can make plans."

"Yes, we definitely need to chat." Desiree gave her a parting hug. "Talk to you soon."

Cynthia returned to the living room. With everyone gone she could finally let her guard down. She only hoped that she was able to hide her suspicions from Jackson until she decided what to do.

She went to the phone and dialed.

Jackson was quiet on the ride back to pick up his car at Lincoln's place. He studied his notes and put them together with what wasn't said, the facial expressions and the body language. Those were the real keys that he'd discovered in his line of work. The mouth could say one thing, but the eyes and body never lied.

"So what did you think?" Lincoln asked, as they pulled up in front of his building. "You've been quiet the whole trip. Anything new?"

Jackson snapped his notebook closed. "Cynthia Hastings is definitely hiding something. She knows much more than she's telling. It may take a little time, but I will find out what it is."

Cynthia drove her car into the parking garage adjacent to her mother's co-op and hurried to the front door. She didn't stop when the doorman called out his greetings and tried to tell her something that was probably more gossip than truth. She didn't have time today. Her mother always went to the theater on Wednesdays with her theater group. Cynthia wanted to get in and out of the apartment.

She gave the elevator attendant the floor number and tried to concentrate on calming her jangling nerves. The elevator doors swooshed open and Cynthia stepped out into the lush corridor. For a moment she stood there debating if what she was about to do was the right thing. She was torn between her obligation to her friend and the blood ties to her mother.

Maybe she was wrong. Maybe when she walked into the suite she'd realize that she'd blown things out of proportion and that with the stress of everything that had gone on, her imagination was working overtime.

Consoling herself with that thought, she walked the length of the hallway to her mother's apartment door.

Just as she was putting her key in the lock, it was pulled open and Jackson Trent stood in front of her.

Startled, she needed a moment for his sudden appearance to register. "What are you doing here?" she demanded, getting her thoughts together.

"I'd hoped to meet your mother, but I did have a chance to speak with Mary." He gave Cynthia a long, penetrating stare.

Her face grew warm under his close scrutiny and she felt as if he could read her mind. She jutted her chin forward the way she'd seen her mother do hundreds of times when dealing with "help."

"You didn't say anything about coming here when we spoke barely more than an hour ago," she challenged. "And what right do you have to speak to my mother's staff?"

"I would think that you would be more than happy to see that I was on the job—especially since it has to do with your friend and former employer." He gave her the barest of grins. "Besides, part of doing my job is not always informing one suspect what I plan to do with another."

Cynthia blinked rapidly, certain that she didn't hear him correctly. "Suspect? Are you saying that I'm a suspect—that my mother is a suspect?"

"Until a case is closed, Ms. Hastings, everyone is a suspect." He stepped past her. "I'm sure we'll be talking again. Have a good day." He turned to Mary, who'd remained mum during the brief exchange. "Thank you for all your help." He walked down the hall to the elevator.

Cynthia turned on Mary. "What did he say to you? What did he want to know?" She swept into the apartment.

Mary closed the door behind her. "He asked me a lot of questions about your mother." She folded her arms and stood her ground.

Cynthia whirled toward her. "What kind of questions?"

"He wanted to know how long I've worked here, the kind of people who come and go, her friends, her relationship with you."

Cynthia's eyes flashed. "What did you tell him?"

"I told him the truth, Ms. Cynthia. I told him that your mother is a difficult woman, to put it mildly, and that the relationship she has with you is shameful."

"How could you do that—air the family's laundry to a perfect stranger?" Her voice rose in pitch. "How dare you betray Mother when she's been nothing but good to you all these years?" Her cheeks were crimson.

Mary tossed back her dark head of tight curls and laughed long and loud. She put her hands on her narrow hips and squinted her eyes.

"Who you think you foolin'? Not me! I been here as

long as you've been on this earth. I see things. I hear things. You think I'm blind and stupid? You think I don't know what goes on around here, the things that your mother does, the way she talks to and treats you? Your mother would do whatever was in her power to get what she wanted, no matter who it hurt—including you. The real question is, how long are you going to let her walk on you like a doormat and then tell *you* to clean yourself up?"

Cynthia's breaths came in short bursts as she danced between fury and desolation. Everything that Mary said about her mother was true and then some. But the reality was, Mary, whatever her good intentions might be, had crossed the invisible line that people of wealth and power draw in the sand. As much as she might dislike her mother and abhor the things she'd done, blue blood still ran in her veins. The hired help was just that, and their loyalty was solely to their employer.

"I will be speaking with my mother about your insubordination," Cynthia said, sounding so much like her mother to her own ears that she was momentarily stunned. "In the meantime," she continued, adapting the haughty tone from years of indoctrination, "I want you to leave. If Mother decides to bring you back, that will be her choice."

Mary pulled off her apron and looked at Cynthia with pity and disappointment in her eyes.

"I always believed that one of these days you'd be strong enough to finally break away from your mother's grasp." She lowered her head and shook it. "But I see you haven't or can't." She looked into Cynthia's startled blue eyes. "Don't become your mother, no matter how much you want her to love you."

Mary folded the apron and placed it on the hall table, then opened the closet and took out her purse and light jacket. She looked at Cynthia one last time and walked out.

Cynthia stared at the closed door with Mary's damning words reverberating in her head. She was not like her mother! She wasn't. She swallowed back the knot that was forming in her throat and took what she'd come for.

Without giving herself a chance to change her mind, she stuck it in her purse. She took a quick look around, then hurried out before her mother returned.

Chapter 38

"Nothing like a man who knows his way around a kitchen," Desiree said, easing behind Lincoln and wrapping her arms around his narrow waist.

He glanced at her over his right shoulder. "I learned early on that the quickest way to your heart was a good home-cooked meal, followed by rock-your-world sex."

"And not necessarily in that order," she said with a giggle.

"Be careful or we may have dessert before the main course."

"That's not such a bad idea," she cooed, rising up on tiptoes to kiss the back of his neck. "What are you fixing anyway? Need some help?" She tried to get a peek in the pots and he swatted her hand away.

"Grilled salmon with my *very* special sauce."

"Oh, not the *very* special sauce," she said, rolling her eyes upward in delight.

Lincoln chuckled. "Wild rice…but not too wild. Fresh string beans."

"How fresh?" she said, feigning deep interest.

"As fresh as your scent when you step out of the shower."

She nodded in approval. "That's pretty darn fresh. What else?"

He turned from the stove and pulled her to stand in between his opened legs. He let his eyes roll over her for a moment, delighting in what he saw.

His voice was a low throb. "I figured for dessert we could adjourn to the master bedroom and sample the new sheets that I put on the bed just for you."

Her left brow arched and her mouth fought back a grin. "Just for me…well…" She reached around him and turned off the pots and the oven. "Seems to me we might have a little time before the main course, so I was thinking we might go straight for the dessert. I know that always works up my appetite." Her fingers played with his belt buckle until she unfastened it and released the zipper.

A sudden dark hunger drifted across Lincoln's eyes like clouds before a major storm.

"I don't think we'll make it to sample the sheets." He eased her back until her legs brushed the table. "I always had a thing for a woman who knew how to make it easily accessible for a man," he whispered, kissing her neck and pushing the oversized T-shirt of his that she wore up over her hips to reveal pure, fresh nakedness beneath.

Desiree grinned mischievously. "And I truly admire a man who knows his way around an accessible woman," she said in a husky voice. She clasped his hardened sex in her hand, running her thumb across the sensitive tip, and moaned right along with him.

He lifted her onto the table and just like in the scene from *The Postman Only Rings Twice,* he tossed the table's contents to the floor, spread her warm brown thighs and found his way home.

Sitting Indian style in the center of Lincoln's king-size bed, with their dinner plates filled to the brim, Lincoln and Desiree finally had their meal.

"That was new and different," Desiree said, before lifting a piece of salmon to her mouth.

"We have the rest of our lives to experiment in new places with new tricks."

"I'm looking forward to it."

Lincoln's eyes found hers. "Are you sure that spending your life with me is what you want?"

"Yes, I am."

"Then this calls for a toast!" He set his tray aside and reached for the bottle of wine on the nightstand. He filled the glasses and handed one to Desiree.

"To our future—together—no matter what it may bring," he said, raising his glass.

Desiree touched her glass to his. "To the future." She took a sip and put her glass down. She was thoughtful for a moment. "Linc, why do you think Jackson said what he did about Cynthia hiding something?" She filled her fork with wild rice.

"I'm sure he has his reasons. Although I fail to see what Cynthia would gain by hiding anything. After all, she lost her job, too—not that she really needs it, from what you've told me and from what I've seen."

Desiree nodded in agreement. "Exactly." She pushed out a frustrated breath. "It's all just so ugly. I want it to be over so I can put it all behind me and move on with my life." She chewed on her salmon. "And all those questions about her mother. What was that about?"

"Got me. But your friend Allison said he was good, so let's just let him do his job and not worry about it."

"You're right. I hope Cynthia wasn't too upset or offended by some of his questions."

"I'm sure she wasn't. She seems like a pretty tough lady."

"Well, I'm going to go and see her tomorrow. We can talk then."

"I didn't want to tell you before with everything going on, but I'm going to need to get back to The Port. I have some contractors coming in to discuss some work that needs to be done and I can't do it by phone."

"Oh…when do you have to leave?"

"Friday morning."

"All right. I'll just stay here until you get back."

"No, you won't. You're coming with me. Until all this business is straightened out and Carl Hampton is where he belongs, you're not getting out of my sight. No discussions."

"Lincoln, I'll be fine."

"I'm sure you will be, but you're coming anyway. End of story."

She pursed her lips but opted not to protest any further. Truthfully, she was getting used to being with Lincoln again and she wasn't ready for the spell to be broken.

"If you insist," she said, pretending to grumble.

"Now, that's how I like my woman," he teased, "soft and pliable." He ran his hand along the curve of her waist.

"Oh, really now?" she tossed back. She put her food tray down on the floor next to the bed. Then on her hands and knees crept toward him like a lioness hunting for lunch. "Funny thing is," she said, lowering the timbre of her voice, "I like my man just the opposite."

Lincoln's devilish grin was filled with promise. "Hmm." He pulled her toward him until she was stretched out along the length of his supine body. "Then we'll have to do something about that. Won't we?"

"Yes," she purred, flicking her tongue across the warm flesh of his chest. "We will."

"I think we need a bigger shower," Lincoln said over the rush of water. He languidly spread body wash across Desiree's back and rubbed it with a soft sponge.

She turned to face him, pressing her soapy breasts against his chest.

"I like the intimate feel of this one."

He pointed the shower head in her direction and she slowly turned in a circle to rinse off.

"Whatever the lady wants." He held his face up to the pulsing water and let it splash all over him.

Desiree stepped out of the shower and reached for a towel hanging on the warming rack. As she passed the towel across her face she was no longer standing in Lincoln's bathroom in Manhattan. She was in their old apartment in Fort Green, Brooklyn....

She was in a hurry as usual, rushing to get ready to go see a Patti LaBelle concert at Lincoln Center. It was Valentine's Day.

She and Lincoln hadn't been out for months. Between his work and her schedule they'd hardly had the time or energy to do much more than have dinner and fall into bed at night.

"We need a break," Lincoln had said weeks earlier as they'd snuggled in bed, thankful for the body warmth against the chill of the frigid outdoors that constantly knocked against their windows begging to get in. "And you need to take it easy in your condition."

She peeked up at him from above the tip of the down comforter that was up to her nose.

"Oh, you mean the condition you put me in," she teased. "You sound just like my grandmother. I'm only four months pregnant, not disabled. Women work right up until the last minute these days."

"That's all those other women." He pulled her close and placed his hand on her rounded belly. "My woman is special. And just to show you how special…remember how many times you told me you wanted to see Patti when she was in concert?"

She sat up, the chill forgotten. "Zillions."

"Well, I have two tickets for her special Valentine's Day performance at Lincoln Center."

"Get out!" She beamed in delight and planted a big kiss on his lips. "See, you are a decent guy. I don't care what the *National Enquirer* says about you," she said, laughter ringing in her voice.

"Am I the greatest or what?" he joked, pulling her even closer.

"Hmm, let me check," she said as her head disappeared beneath the covers.

The days leading up to the concert flew by, and before Desiree realized it, Valentine's Day was upon her and as usual she was unorganized and behind schedule.

She fished through her lingerie drawer for a pair of stockings, only to find one lone pair with runs.

"Damn it!" She checked her watch. They were scheduled to leave at seven. It was already six and if she knew Lincoln, he'd be ready to walk out of the door in a half hour.

She contemplated wearing a pantsuit to cover the runs, but of course she hadn't made time to stop at the cleaner's. She'd run out of options and was running out of time.

While Lincoln was in the shower, she put on her coat, grabbed her purse and darted out. She could get a pair of cheap pantyhose from the corner store and be back in a flash.

Her next-door neighbor's five-year-old son, Sean, was forever dropping one of his action figures in the hall or on the stairs. Desiree generally made it a point to be on the lookout and had on more than several occasions spoken with Sean's mother about it with only intermittent results.

Tonight her mind was on getting to the store and back before Lincoln started with his impatient pacing. That and a long-overdue night out on the town with her man. She didn't see the black Hot Wheels racing car on the third step. And the next thing she knew she was sliding down the stairs. She grabbed the banister to try to break the fall and felt every muscle in her belly scream in protest as her back made contact with the steps on her way down.

Miraculously she didn't go down head over heels. For several moments she lay on the next-to-last step, terrified, expecting the worst. She pulled in long, slow breaths and gingerly rose to her feet, using the railing for support. She took the final two stairs with caution.

On solid ground she made a mental assessment of her body, inch by inch. Her heart was racing out of control and there was a dull throb in her back and she was sure she'd bruised her knee. She pressed her hand to her stomach and felt the telltale flutter of life deep in her womb. She released a relieved breath. Her baby was all right.

Taking her time now, she went to the store, picked up her stockings and came back to the apartment.

"Where were you?" Lincoln asked, running a towel across his face as Desiree walked into the bedroom.

"Had to pick up some stockings."

"Well, we need to step on it. You know how tough it is to park around there." He looked at her for a moment. A frown creased his forehead. He stepped closer to her. "Are you feeling okay? Your face looks strained. What's wrong?"

"I'm fine. Really. It's just that I know how much you don't like to rush and I need to get ready, that's all."

He stared into her eyes. "Are you sure? Because if you're not feeling well we don't have to go. Nothing's more important to me than you and our baby."

Desiree forced herself to smile and pressed her finger to his chin. "You worry too much. I'm fine. Now let me go and get ready."

The next thing she remembered was the sound of sirens and looking up into Lincoln's worried face as they rode to the hospital in an ambulance.

"You're going to be all right, Desi," he murmured over and over. He stroked her brow as another cramp tore through her stomach.

But she wasn't fine and she'd never be fine again.

* * *

"Earth to Desiree, earth to Desiree."

Desiree moved the towel from her face, and the room came back into focus. "Huh?"

"A towel, could you pass me one?"

"Sure. Sorry," she said absently. She wrapped her towel around her body, tucking it beneath her arms and walked out of the bathroom.

When Lincoln came out he found her sitting on the side of the bed staring into space.

"What's on your mind?" he asked gently, sensing that she was on the verge of slipping into the private sanctuary of her mind where she shut out everyone and everything, including him. It had ruined their relationship once, when they didn't confront it head-on. Not this time.

"Talk to me. Whatever it is." He tightened the towel around his waist and waited. "And don't tell me it's nothing."

Desiree glanced up at him, clear-eyed and resolute.

"I was thinking about the day I lost the baby."

His stomach muscles tightened. He didn't move. He wanted her to talk.

"I've always wondered, if I had told you right away instead of pretending that everything was fine, would the baby have had a chance?" She folded her hands in her lap. "I don't know and I guess I will never know. But what I did to you was wrong. I shut you out and grieved alone as if your loss was not as great as mine.

And I lost five years of being able to be loved by you and me loving you back."

By degrees his tensed muscles began to relax. He walked toward her, took her hand and pulled her to her feet.

"It's like I told you, baby, we have the rest of our lives to love each other." He kissed the tip of her nose. "And I intend to use every minute of it." He tickled her side until she giggled. "Except for the next few hours. I have some business to take care of at the bank."

"That's fine actually. I wanted to visit Cynthia anyway."

"I'll drop you off on my way and you can call my cell when you've finished your girl talk and I'll come and pick you up."

"Let me give her a call and make sure she'll be home."

Chapter 39

Probably the last thing she needed to do today was meet with Desiree. But she couldn't come up with a good enough excuse, especially after telling her how much they needed to get together and catch up. Besides, Desiree said that she and Lincoln would be heading back to Sag Harbor for a few days. Had she said no, it would have seemed odd and definitely suspicious.

Cynthia glanced at the statue that she'd put on her dresser. As much as she didn't want to believe it, the statue was one of Desiree's creations. Her signature was on the bottom.

She remembered when it had been purchased. Desiree took it off the inventory the very same day as the fire. Why did her mother have it? What was her connection? She didn't want to imagine. But what kept her up all night long was a recurring nightmare. She was standing atop a great mountain. Below was her mother being chased by an angry mob—all the people she'd walked over, used, or ruined. Her mother was running toward her, trying to get up the mountain to safety.

Within her grasp, Cynthia for the first time had the power to decide her mother's fate. If she reached out her hand, she would be saved. If not...

In some versions, Cynthia rescued her mother and Eleanor showered her with all her withheld love and affection and Cynthia reveled in it.

In other versions, she simply stood there, motionless, and watched her mother become engulfed by the crowd that ran after her.

Cynthia looked down at the statue that she gripped in her hand. Every fiber of her being told her that her mother was somehow involved in the destruction of the gallery that nearly cost Desiree her life.

She had a choice to make, a choice that would permanently change the course of her relationship with her mother.

"Okay, call me when you're ready for me to pick you up," Lincoln said as he came to a stop in front of Cynthia's building.

She leaned over and kissed his cheek. "Yes, sir. See you later, sir."

"Very funny. Enjoy your visit."

Desiree hopped out and waved as she watched Lincoln drive off. When he was out of sight she went to the front door and rang the bell.

"So tell me about this guy you met," Desiree said as they sat together on the couch.

"I actually met him at a bar."

"You—at a bar! I didn't know you drank."

"I don't. Not really." She reached for her iced tea from the coffee table. "Anyway, by the time we actually met I was pretty wasted. He had to bring me home."

"Cynthia, you're kidding. You got so drunk that you let a perfect stranger bring you home?"

Cynthia squeezed up her face and nodded. "I know. Stupid, right? I could have been a statistic." She took a swallow of her tea. "Anyway, he brought me home, left his number, and I called him the next day. We went out to dinner the other night."

"Hmmph. Is he cute at least?"

Cynthia giggled. "Yeah, in a Clark Kent kind of way."

"Well, you know Clark Kent has that Superman thing going on. So watch out."

They laughed.

"Enough about me. What's been going on with you?"

Desiree sat back against the couch cushions and in a bunch of fits and starts she brought Cynthia up to date on all that had occurred with her rekindling her relationship with Lincoln.

"Wow. Guess you two are meant to be together."

"I think so, too," Desiree said. "I just want all of this

business with the fire and the investigation to be over and done with." She slowly shook her head. "Arson… what kind of person does something like that?"

Cynthia fidgeted in her seat. "Uh, have you heard from Carl?"

Desiree's gaze darted in Cynthia's direction and then away. "I understand he's in the Bahamas," she said, avoiding the question.

"Bahamas! With everything that's going on? Don't you think that's kind of strange?"

"I don't put anything past Carl," she said, the disgust obvious in her voice.

Cynthia frowned. "Did something else happen with Carl?"

"Nothing that I want to talk about at the moment." She sipped from her glass and stared out the window.

Finally Cynthia spoke, breaking the silence. "What are your plans? I mean what are you going to do about your work?"

Desiree shrugged. "I'm just past the nightmares," she said in a faraway voice. "I haven't been able to paint." She shrugged. "So…I really don't know. Hopefully one day I'll be able to go back to it without feeling like I want to scream." She stretched, then checked her watch. "I need to call Lincoln."

"You can use the phone in the bedroom."

"Thanks." She got up and walked toward the bed-room.

She entered the room and spotted the phone by the

bed. She sat on the side of the bed and punched in Lincoln's cell phone number. While she waited for the call to connect she looked around the room and suddenly her entire body went cold.

Sitting on top of Cynthia's dresser was the statue from the gallery. The same one that the woman purchased—the day of the fire.

Her heart began to thump as images ran rampant in her head and her thoughts raced, trying to make sense of it all.

"Hello? Hello? Desi."

She took a deep breath and slowly walked to the dresser.

"Lincoln," she whispered and peered toward the partially opened bedroom door for any sign of Cynthia.

"Desi, what is it? Are you all right?"

"The statue…"

"What statue? What are you talking about?"

"It's here in Cynthia's bedroom. The statue from my gallery," she hissed.

"I'm not understanding you."

"It's the same statue that the woman bought that day. The same woman we ran into in Sag Harbor who swore she didn't know me. Why is it here?"

"I'm coming for you right now. Don't say anything to Cynthia. I'll call Jackson. I want you to leave. Now. Meet me outside."

"Okay, okay," she said, suddenly more afraid than confused. "I'll meet you out front."

"I'll be there in ten minutes."

Desiree hung up the phone just as Cynthia poked her head in the door.

"Did you get him?"

Desiree swallowed. "Yes, uh, he said he was in the neighborhood. He'll be outside in a few minutes."

Cynthia frowned. "Is something wrong? You look upset."

"I'm fine. Just getting a headache."

"Oh, let me get you something."

"It's okay. Don't trouble yourself." She hurried out of the room, took her purse from the couch and turned to Cynthia. "I'll call you when I get back."

Cynthia gave her a long look. "Sure. I'll walk you to the door."

"Take care," Desiree said.

Cynthia's hand suddenly covered hers. "You do the same."

Desiree's heart leaped to her throat. "Thanks. Bye."

Cynthia watched as Desiree left the building, knowing that what had sent her running was what she'd discovered in her bedroom.

Slowly she closed the door. Desiree was an intelligent, resourceful woman. Cynthia had no doubt that if she hadn't put the pieces together already she would very shortly. And when Desiree did, Cynthia would be prepared.

Chapter 40

Carl's driver was waiting for him when he landed at JFK Airport.

"I'm going straight to the office," he said without preamble. He settled himself in the car and contemplated his next move.

He'd lost his perspective, he thought, as the Belt Parkway opened out in front of him. He'd allowed raw emotion to drive his decisions and he'd made one mistake after another as a result. He didn't realize how single-minded, power-driven and greedy he'd become until he saw himself through Desiree's eyes that night. The fear and disgust that lashed back at him haunted him in a way that none of his other under-the-table dealings had ever done.

He knew that he'd crossed the line—his own line—and he couldn't look himself in the face knowing what he'd become.

What he'd almost done was reprehensible, but what Desiree had done was more startling. She hadn't reported it. That much he knew from his contacts in the police department. It was when he'd gotten the call from Jake about the turmoil back home that he finally realized that Desiree had inadvertently given him a chance—a chance to do the right thing or keep living the way he'd been living.

Carl reached into his jacket pocket and took out his cell phone. He dialed Jake Foxx.

"Just listen and don't ask questions." He laid out what he wanted done.

"Are you sure it's the same one?" Lincoln asked as he weaved in and out of midtown Manhattan traffic.

"I know my own work," she snapped and immediately regretted it. "I'm sorry. Didn't mean to take your head off." She patted his thigh, then bit down on her thumbnail. "But you know there's something not right, Linc." Her brows knitted together. "Cynthia had to know that statue was in her bedroom in plain sight and that I'd see it and know it was mine. It's a one-of-a-kind piece."

"Okay, let's think about this. Cynthia has the statue, which she must have gotten from that woman. And the woman just happened to come to the gallery the very day that it burns down."

Desiree pressed her lips together and nodded slowly, allowing the pieces to fall in place. "And Cynthia wanted me to see it and connect the dots." She turned to Lincoln. "That says to me that Cynthia is not the guilty one, but she knows who is."

"And she doesn't want to tell you directly."

"Because that person is—"

"Her mother," they said in unison.

"Turn around," Desiree said. "I want to go back."

Lincoln threw her a glance even as he checked traffic and made a sharp U-turn. "I was hoping you were going to say that."

Carl walked into the conference room. The management team and the accountant were all present as requested.

"Thank you all for rearranging your schedules on such short notice." He walked to the head of the table, adjusted his navy blue pin-striped jacket and sat down in his executive chair. "There have been a lot of rumors and innuendos running rampant through the company. My name and the reputation of the company have been dragged through the mud in every paper in the city." He cleared his throat and lifted his chin. "The things you've heard are true. Hampton Enterprises is in financial trouble, serious trouble, and has been for quite some time."

Loud murmurs and looks of disbelief ran around the table. The accountant worked his tie back and forth to loosen it as if he were being strangled.

"As of today, I'm resigning as president and CEO of Hampton Enterprises and immediately filing for bankruptcy." His voice cracked but he continued. "I'm going to dissolve all of my personal assets to try to offset the debt."

There was another series of shouts and banging on the table.

"What about us?" one of the managers shouted over the others.

"Quiet down!" Carl slammed his fist on the table. "Do any of you think this is easy? This is my company." He poked at his chest and glared at each of them in turn. "I built this company from nothing, gave some of you jobs when you still needed to have your noses wiped." His voice lowered. "I came into this business full of energy and idealism. Over the years I allowed greed and power to control me, to replace the very things this business was built on.

"Hampton Enterprises owes millions more than it's taking in. And the loans are long overdue."

"Is there any truth to the rumor about the fire?" one of the other managers asked.

The room fell silent.

He looked at each of them. "I didn't know it at the time, but I know now. Yes."

Desiree clasped Lincoln's hand as they stood in front of Cynthia's building waiting for her to answer the door.

It opened and Cynthia stood in front of them with a look of acceptance in her blue eyes.

"I knew you would come back," she said in a monotone. She turned and walked inside. Desiree and Lincoln followed.

When they entered the living room, the damning statue sat in the center of the coffee table.

Lance rose from the couch. He stretched out his hand toward Cynthia, which she took.

Desiree looked from one to the other and tried to figure out where Lance fit into all of it.

Cynthia read her thoughts. "Lance is here to make sure that I don't do anything stupid, like I'd intended to do. And what was that? Take the blame for something my mother did," she said, answering her own question.

Desiree lowered herself to a chair, relieved that her hunch about Cynthia had been correct, but pained for the angst that Cynthia must have gone through and was going through to come to this moment.

Inhaling deeply, Cynthia told them about the fight she and her mother had, her knocking over the statue on the way out, how Jackson's questions made her really think about it, her trip back to her mother's apartment and bringing the statue to her own apartment.

Cynthia turned briefly to Lance. "Some stupid part of me wanted to take the blame for everything, knowing that my mother was somehow behind it in some way."

"Why, Cynthia?" Desiree asked, totally perplexed.

"I thought that if I did, it would show her how much I loved her and maybe she would love me back."

"Oh, Cyn," Desiree said, empathy and hurt welling in her voice. She got up and went to her side, taking a seat next to her. "Sacrificing yourself, your beliefs for the approval and love of others will never give you what you hope to gain." She looked at Lincoln for a long moment and her own life and decision came into crystal-clear focus. "I wasted five years of my life and countless others trying to be the person my family thought I should be. I lost Lincoln and a part of myself in the process. But like you, I got the chance to make my life right and do what was right for me. It's hard, but you won't regret it."

Cynthia blinked back tears and gripped Lance's hand a bit tighter. "I hope not."

Lincoln's cell phone rang. "Excuse me." He stood and walked out into the hallway and listened with disbelief and fascination to what Jackson had uncovered.

Allison Wakefield's byline appeared beneath the headline: NEW YORK SOCIALITE AND PROMINENT BUSINESS TYCOON BEHIND INSURANCE SCAM—POSSIBLY LINKED TO ATTEMPTED MURDER OF LOCAL ARTIST. The article went on to outline Eleanor Hastings and Carl Hampton's longstanding business agreements spanning a decade. Hastings provided seed money for many of his enterprises through intermediaries such as Sylvester Ward, according to information obtained by investigator Jackson Trent. According to Trent, Hastings recouped her investments from nonpaying clients by torching their buildings and obtaining the insurance money. There were indications that yet another unidentified woman was also involved.

Desiree put the paper down on the kitchen table after reading the article to Lincoln.

"What makes a person that greedy, that evil?" she asked.

Lincoln stretched out his long legs beneath the table. "Money or lack of it has toppled everything from marriages to corporations to whole nations. Money is equated with power, and power can corrupt even the best of us. I'm just glad that Cynthia wasn't involved."

"So am I. I feel so bad for her and what she was willing to sacrifice."

"Cynthia is a tough girl. She would have to be to have a mother like Eleanor Hastings. I'm sure she will be fine."

Desiree sighed. "Yeah, she will." She pushed up from the table. "Well, if we plan to get to Sag Harbor anytime today we need to get moving. And I want to stop by Rachel's place to pick up some things."

"I thought you had everything here."

"Almost everything." She smiled. "I think when we get to the shore I might feel like painting."

Chapter 41

With each passing day, as summer slowly turned to fall, Desiree spent the daylight hours on the beach, in the center of town, or perched on the stones behind her cabin—painting.

It was as if the floodgates had opened and all the creative energy that she held inside for so long flowed from her. Her images were sharp, brilliant and filled with life, one outshining the next.

Eleanor and Carl had been indicted and their trial was set for early the following year. Cynthia and Lance were doing well and she'd talked about opening a small shop of her own in the Village. Desiree was happy for her.

She put the finishing touches on a landscape that

she'd been working on and set it to the side. She looked out toward the main house and saw Lincoln's Navigator pulling into the drive. She smiled and fingered the diamond on her left hand. Lincoln had kept the ring, and one week ago, over dinner on the beach, he'd asked her to marry him—again. This time, she was sure, this time she knew she was going into it with her mind and her heart wide open and ready to receive the love he had to offer.

She watched him as he made his way up the walk toward her, and her heart filled with warmth. She loved Lincoln, loved him with every fiber of her being. Fate brought him back into her life, but it was Lincoln who challenged her to face her fears, to open herself to possibility, dare to dream.

Desiree put down her brush and wiped her hands on her smock, and she wondered if tonight when they lay together it would be a good time to tell him about another dream that had become reality. She pressed her hands to her stomach and waited for her man.

* * * * *

A new trilogy from *USA TODAY*
bestselling author

KAYLA PERRIN

Home is where the *Hart* is....

ALWAYS IN MY HEART	SURRENDER MY HEART	HEART TO HEART

Available May 2012	*Available June 2012*	*Available July 2012*

THREE HARTS.  THREE LOVES.
THE REUNION OF A LIFETIME.

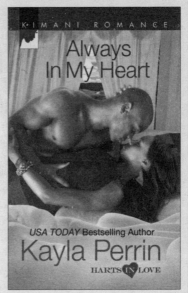

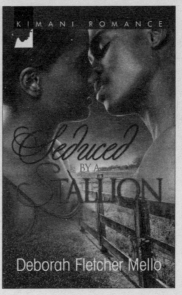

REQUEST YOUR FREE BOOKS!

2 FREE NOVELS
PLUS 2 FREE GIFTS!

KIMANI™
ROMANCE

Love's ultimate destination!

YES! Please send me 2 FREE Kimani™ Romance novels and my 2 FREE gifts (gifts are worth about $10). After receiving them, if I don't wish to receive any more books, I can return the shipping statement marked "cancel." If I don't cancel, I will receive 4 brand-new novels every month and be billed just $4.94 per book in the U.S. or $5.49 per book in Canada. That's a saving of at least 21% off the cover price. It's quite a bargain! Shipping and handling is just 50¢ per book in the U.S. and 75¢ per book in Canada.* I understand that accepting the 2 free books and gifts places me under no obligation to buy anything. I can always return a shipment and cancel at any time. Even if I never buy another book, the two free books and gifts are mine to keep forever.

168/368 XDN FEJR

Name	(PLEASE PRINT)
Address	Apt. #
City	State/Prov.	Zip/Postal Code

Signature (if under 18, a parent or guardian must sign)

Mail to the **Reader Service**:
IN U.S.A.: P.O. Box 1867, Buffalo, NY 14240-1867
IN CANADA: P.O. Box 609, Fort Erie, Ontario L2A 5X3

Not valid for current subscribers to Kimani Romance books.

Want to try two free books from another line?
Call 1-800-873-8635 or visit www.ReaderService.com.

* Terms and prices subject to change without notice. Prices do not include applicable taxes. Sales tax applicable in N.Y. Canadian residents will be charged applicable taxes. Offer not valid in Quebec. This offer is limited to one order per household. All orders subject to credit approval. Credit or debit balances in a customer's account(s) may be offset by any other outstanding balance owed by or to the customer. Please allow 4 to 6 weeks for delivery. Offer available while quantities last.

Your Privacy—The Reader Service is committed to protecting your privacy. Our Privacy Policy is available online at www.ReaderService.com or upon request from the Reader Service.

We make a portion of our mailing list available to reputable third parties that offer products we believe may interest you. If you prefer that we not exchange your name with third parties, or if you wish to clarify or modify your communication preferences, please visit us at www.ReaderService.com/consumerschoice or write to us at Reader Service Preference Service, P.O. Box 9062, Buffalo, NY 14269. Include your complete name and address.

KROM11B

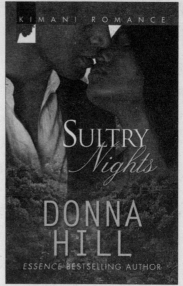